CLANSMAN OF ANDOR

Cleve glanced about. He was adrift with no weapons, no clothing, not even a strip of leather he might somehow turn into a means of defense. He considered diving and striking out for the opposite shore, but could Doralan Andrah's body, which he now inhabited, swim?

He had no time to think. Th [illegible] d
natives were [illegible] e
water, bl [illegible]
was that [illegible]
his own B [illegible]

Cleve h [illegible]
arena bene [illegible]
battle the c [illegible]

By the same author
in Magnum Books

MESSENGER OF ZHUVASTOU
THE CASTLE KEEPS

ANDREW J. OFFUTT

Clansman of Andor

MAGNUM BOOKS
Methuen Paperbacks Ltd

A Magnum Book

CLANSMAN OF ANDOR
ISBN 0 417 03020 7

First published 1976
by Dell Publishing Co. Inc, New York
Magnum edition published 1978

Magnum Books are published
by Methuen Paperbacks Ltd
11 New Fetter Lane, London EC4P 4EE

Made and printed in Great Britain
by Hazell Watson & Viney Ltd,
Aylesbury, Bucks

CONTENTS

PART ONE

Robert Cleve/Doralan Andrah

PROLOGUE

The Cleve of Earth

'My name is Robert Cleve. I've come in response to your advertisement.'

The bespectacled man in the brown suit nodded, smiled. 'No ties, Mr Cleve? None? No care for death?'

Cleve shrugged: a tall man with icy gray eyes and a great pile of red-brown hair. 'No ties. I have no intention of dying anyway soon, but I have no fear of death. I also possess a willingness, as you said, to face anything. What is it I must face?'

The other man smiled. 'That which is hardest to face, Robert Cleve: the Unknown. Be patient. One should never rush toward a tryst with possible death. We have processed the application you submitted three weeks ago, and we have investigated you. That is why you received a reply from us. We find that you are a highly intelligent man, impetuous, with a love of adventure. You exercise both your mind and your body, to keep them both in perfect condition, in accord with the ancient Greek concept. You also seem impervious to vanity . . . I do not mind telling you that you are our most distinguished applicant to date. We are delighted, Mr Cleve. We have a need for you . . . or rather, *someone* has.'

Robert Cleve pulled back the chair across the desk from the bespectacled man and sat in it. He crossed one long leg over the other. 'Since you forgot to invite me to sit, Mr Gordon, I felt sure you'd not mind my inviting myself.'

'That sort of manner will serve you in good stead where you will go, Mr Cleve, should you agree to join us. We learned that you have a tendency to sneer at civilized conventions.'

Cleve shrugged again; shrugged, and did not trouble himself to answer. 'What do you mean, *someone* has need of me?'

Gordon smiled. 'Well, not exactly of you, Mr Cleve. Not of your body. Someone has a need for your mind.'

Cleve looked about without apparent consternation, or indeed, any visible reaction. 'Am I then in a hospital specializing in brain surgery? Am I to have my head cut from my shoulders, or merely my brain from my head?'

'Neither, Robert Cleve.' Gordon's smile had broadened. 'Neither. But first, may I ask you to place your agreement in writing?' He bent slightly forward to place a piece of paper on the desk before Cleve. With his other hand he extended a pen.

After gazing at him a moment, Cleve also bent slightly to examine the sheet of bond. It was a form; there were but a few lines printed upon it, with a space for his signature above the heavy black line.

'Hm. I seem to be agreeing that I have no ties, that my death will discommode no one, that I have no fear of death, and absolve your organization of any responsibility or blame or lawsuit in the event of my demise.' He looked up, and the gray eyes were like ice in Arctic seas. 'Either you are an ass, Mr Gordon, or you must believe that I am. If I sign this now, without explanation, then you might well draw a pistol from a drawer of your desk and shoot me dead – with perfect impunity.'

Gordon gazed at him, his eyes hugely magnified behind his round spectacles. He blinked, and he added. 'Yes, sir. Quite right. Aside from the fact that I have no pistol in my desk drawer, I well might do just as you say. You refuse to sign it?'

Cleve stared. 'Fascinating,' he said, slowly and quietly. 'Mr Gordon, I believe you are serious. Might I be favored with the answers to a few questions?'

'Possibly,' Gordon said, just as quietly. 'I cannot promise. Perhaps I can answer them before they are posed. You admit to boredom by answering our ad, and attest to it by your presence here. I assure you that if you sign that piece of paper, you will either face danger or flee from it, and worse danger by far than you faced on your safari in Africa or during your distinguished military service or on your recent tiger shoot in India. Perhaps we make too much mention of death. If you die, it will not be by my hand or through the machinations of this organization, for you shall first have agreed to where we wish to send you. If you die, it will be a fighting death, although the weapons will not be firearms. You will have adventures, Mr Cleve – yes, plural, and in abundance. The opportunity for greatness – although your friends will never know of your achievements. And the opportunity to die. In which case your friends will never be certain. For once you agree, Robert Cleve – and that is a matter yet to be discussed, subsequent to your signing that paper – once you agree, you vanish from this world.'

'We have a twofold agreement to make, then?'

'Threefold. Further questions?'

Robert Cleve pushed Gordon's pen back at him, and for a brief moment the older man looked disappointed. But then Cleve was withdrawing a gold pen from his pocket, screwing out the point, and quickly signing the document. He pushed it across to Gordon without change in his facial expression or posture, which was rather stiffly erect.

'The second, Gordon?'

Gordon opened a drawer of his desk, without taking his eyes off Cleve's face. He wiped the signed agreement into the drawer. 'You did not flinch when I opened the drawer,' he said, and it was a question.

Cleve did not reply. He raised one shoulder slightly in a shrug.

'I am aware of your habit of ignoring statements and questions which you feel require no comment, Robert Cleve. But – please comment.'

Cleve gazed steadily at him. 'I did not expect you to withdraw a pistol, Mr Gordon. I believed you. But – had you done so, you would have died first.'

'The pen?'

'The pen.'

'Highly illegal.'

'Your investigation has undoubtedly uncovered the fact that I am what might be called an atavist, Mr Gordon. I believe in personal justice. The swifter the better.'

Gordon smiled again. 'Yes,' he breathed, and his tone indicated he had received confirmation of that which he already knew. 'You really don't belong in our society.' He extended a second piece of paper, another almost-blank form.

Cleve read it swiftly, shrugged, signed it. In doing so, he agreed that, should he refuse to carry on once he'd heard Gordon's proposal, he would tell no one anything concerning the organization of which Gordon was a part.

'State your proposition, Mr Gordon.' Thus spoke the eyes of Robert Cleve; Cleve spoke not a word.

'Believe what I will say, Mr Cleve, or refuse to believe, as you wish. Your body will remain here, in a tank reduced to a temperature you would not believe, by liquid nitrogen. Your body, I say, will remain here. But your mind will not. *If you agree*, Robert Cleve, your mind will enter the body of Doralan Andrah of Andor.'

'Who?'

'Doralan Andrah, Mr Cleve. His body is athletic, young, and in fine condition. Nor is he ill-favored, and he has position. You will be in sole control. He is in a position to render a great service to many poeple, to his world. But he cannot. He never will. He is dying. He has a brain tumor. It will never be diagnosed, much less cured, where he is. It is not surprising that you do not recognize the name Doralan Andrah. Nor, I assure you, have you ever heard of him. He is not of this planet.'

Cleve gazed at the man across the glass-topped desk in the oak-paneled office behind a glass door. 'You know, Gordan, you *look* like a sane man. Thus I cannot question your sanity, not yet, not aloud. But . . . you realize my thoughts. Somewhere, you are telling me, on another planet, is a man named Door-Alan Andruh. He is in a position to do some great deed or deeds, but will not, because he's laid low of a brain tumor. It will not be diagnosed, you say, and I assume you mean that his planet has not progressed to the diagnosing of such a disorder. Also, you mentioned before that I should have no firearms. Because you are for some reason interested in Mr Andruh or his success, you propose to place my body in a refrigerated sort of suspended animation – a sort of cryobiological stasis, isn't it? – and hurl my – my brain across space to enter his body?'

'First, it would be "Mr Doralan," not "Mr Andrah." The first name is the patronymic, in most areas on Andor. Secondly, I am impressed with your remembering what I said before and keying it in. You are correct. No firearms, no medical science as we know it. Furthermore, there will *never* be firearms on Andor, unless they are carried in – there seems to be no saltpeter on the planet.' Gordon leaned back and took great care in fitting, precisely, the tips of his fingers together. 'Despite your dubious tone, Mr Cleve, you have stated it precisely. Shall I continue?'

'Continue,' Robert Cleve said, leaning forward.

Chapter One

The Doralan of Doralan

Robert Cleve awoke. For a moment he lay still, staring up at darkness.

No, not darkness. A night sky, yes; but a sky alight with stars strewn like scintillant gems upon a jeweler's case of black velvet. A sky lit further by three baubles much larger than the others, one rather greenish, the others pale and silver-glowing. Robert Cleve's eyes rolled from one to the other.

The stars were totally unfamiliar; nowhere was there any pattern or conformation he recognized. The larger jewels were . . . moons.

Robert Cleve frowned. Robert Cleve? No. He was not Robert Cleve.

He was Doralan Andrah, Grof ul rodan Doralan.

And this was not Earth. This was Andor, a word meaning 'home dirt,' as its reversed spelling, 'rodan,' meant 'home group' or 'clan.' He lay on the ground, in a blanket, just beside a tent which he knew was in the Mountains of Mist in the land of Elgain, a short distance from the walled city of Mor: 'High.'

And Mor needed him. Elgain needed him.

Robert Cleve, Doralan Andrah, pushed back the blankets and winced at the sudden chill, although it was a warm night. He rose, noticing that his coppery body was muscular, powerful, and hairless, although his Andoran memory told him he had hair aplenty on his head, black and glossy as polished coal. It was drawn back and bound with a band of silver into a single warrior's club on his back. He noticed, too, that his body was stiff, cramped. He'd lain too long idle, and the fever had tensed and knotted his muscles. Well, the activity to come would soon get the kinks out!

'Lord Andrah! You're up!' The voice was excited, yet

it did not rise above a whisper. The speaker was shorter, not so muscular, clad in a simple brown tunic and buskins cross-strapped to his knobbly knees. He wore his hair in a bowl cut, and his black moustache drooped. Robert Cleve's brain thought a smile; Doralan Andrah's face smiled at the other man.

'Of course I'm up. The fever has left me, Biyah, and the illness. I'm as well as you,' the man called grof, or lord chieftain, said. Doralan's voice was firm, sonorous; Robert Cleve liked it: 'How long have I lain thus?'

While his memories were Andrah's, the language had been fed into him via hypnotape, and he had a better vocabulary than his host. But – naturally – Doralan Andrah's mind had no idea how long he'd lain ill – or dying.

'Eleven days, O my lord,' Biyah said, so impressed and happy that he used the formalities he never bothered with. 'But are ye sure you're well?'

'A little stiff, Biyah, only a little stiff. Yes, I am fully recovered.'

'Oh, my lord! Daron be thanked – it's a miracle!'

Again the Earthman's brain stretched the Andorite's face into a grin. 'Pai,' he said, using the affirmative word in Andran, the near-universal language on Andor. 'You might indeed call it a miracle, old friend. A miracle is an occurrence whose explanation is beyond our ken, and I assure you, neither of us kens what has taken place within me! Very well, Biyah. I am hungry, and I must know what has happened in the past eleven days. Eleven days! Daron's mercy! Food, Biyah, and talk. What of the clansmen, what of Mor, what of bloody Thran?'

Hurriedly Biyah set out fruits and meat and brown bread and wine from the thick arbors of Valnyra.

'The clansmen, fret, Andrah. They are almost without heart and ready to disband. Restless they are, even fearful, with you ill. Kishen exhorts them, and both he and Shant claim leadership. And –'

'Couldn't wait for me to be dead, much less cold, eh?' Grof Doralan Andrah spoke between savory mouthfuls of lor steak, roasted on a spit over an open fire.

'They were little different when you were well, Andrah. Both want command. Kishen's family is what it is, and of course Shant's sister *is* a witch. They may present more of a problem now that you are thus weakened. Why don't we keep the miracle of your recovery secret for a few days, Andrah, until you've all your strength back?'

'No time, Biyah. I didn't ask about jackals. I want to know about the clans, about Mor.'

Biyah squatted beside the man he'd grown up with in Doralan Keep and served for years; the chieftain, now that his father was dead, of the Clan Doralan: Grof ul rodan Doralan. And now chieftain of the allied clans: Doralan, Starinor, Molderan, and – parts of – Khoramor. He'd been dying, Biyah was certain, of the same cursed brain-evil that had killed old Doralan. But by some miracle, here hunkered Doralan Andrah before him, those gray Doralan eyes fixed on him, the black clutch of hair stirring between the shoulder blades almost invisible in his broad, thick back. He still wore the short, ungirt sleep tunic with its slanting closure. On the right sleeve of the gray garment Biyah had sewn, with his own hands, the black square and silver bhur of Doralan. It was strange, seeing Doralan in sleeves; sleeves bound his powerful arms, and he disliked them. He wore sleeveless jerkins, with the clan patch high on his left chest – when he wore clothing above the waist at all. The young Doralan favored a padded leather harness that left bare most of his torso.

'Of the clansmen, Andrah, there are more. Several more of Clan Khoramor, and even a few Solanans, poor, leaderless vagabonds. Oh, and Khoramor Shansi is here. Hard it's been to keep her from you, with her sorceries. Perhaps she could have cured you as she said, Andrah. But – I trust no sister of Khoramor Shant!'

Cleve/Doralan nodded. His eyes remained on Biyah. As usual, he had eaten heartily; as usual, he drank but little of the pale wine of neighboring Valnyra. No comment was necessary. Biyah spoke sense. He had also been twice asked about Mor, and he had not yet answered, and his grof waited.

'Half the Clan Doralan is in Mor, Andrah. A third of the Morites know; we believe we can be sure of another third. Rumors only has King Thran heard; he's not so much as doubled the guard.'

'Don't call that murderer "king" in my presence, Biyah.' Then Doralan Andrah's face smiled. 'Fat idiot! Smug in his new kingdom he is, smug on his bloody, stolen throne. Well, we'll soon topple him from it! My harness and boots, Biyah, and a leather kirtle – and the Doralan cloak.'

'Please, Andrah. Wait at least until morn.'

The only reply the freeservant received was a steady gaze from those pale eyes. They belonged to the son as they had to the father; 'twas said old Doralan Doralan had skewered more than one foeman with them, freezing him while the Doralan ax swung up and then down to freeze the man forever in his own curdled blood. Biyah believed it not, for the old chieftain had possessed no magic save that of this world, his mind and strength; though truly the eyes had been fearful. Now the son's identical gray ones seemed even firmer, even more piercing than they had been before he'd fallen ill with the brain fever. And Andrah spoke with more ease. Surely it was a miracle; holy Daron favored Doralan!

Biyah rose and hurried into the black-and-silver tent. He was back in moments, to find his young lord naked, the sleep tunic in a pile at his feet. Andrah was performing some strange rite; he had clenched his hands together and seemed to be striving to pull them apart, so that his biceps bunched.

He swung the padded harness about himself: a huge, silver-bossed baldric that passed over his right shoulder and fastened on the left to the thick leather belt slung low on his hips. Both belts secured with silver buckles big as Biyah's palm. The clansman's bhur swung in its thick leather scabbard from Andrah's left hip, a needle-pointed sword long as his arm, with a serrated edge. From the harness depended a strip of leather, decorated and armored with silver bosses, wide as Andrah's hand and nearly as thick. It provided loin armor even for a naked man; in the old days a warrior had had to snatch harness and fling himself into battle, clothed or not, or the clans of Elgain would not exist. Andrah swung the leather kirtle about his hips, buckling it on the right so that it was split all up that side, affording him maximum facility of movement. He drew on the boots as Biyah whirled about him the silver-lined black cloak. Its padded side covered his left arm, and the silver bhur patch of Clan Doralan gleamed there, near his shoulder.

The Doralan of Doralan glanced up at the sky. It was not Earth's sky, but it was more familiar to Robert Cleve now than Earth's. The men of Andor, without compasses, had good reason to know the stars in their triple-mooned sky.

'It isn't too late. Call the algrof,' he said, adding the Andran plural prefix 'al' to the word for clan leader.

'Andrah . . . Lord . . .'

'I am fine, Biyah. Stop worrying and nagging. But – send me Stek first.' The young Grof of Doralan smiled. 'Armed.'

Biyah nodded, cheered that his lord and friend would at least have at his side the biggest and most loyal of Doralan warriors. He hurried into the darkness.

Robert Cleve's mind directed Doralan Andrah's body to take several paces forward. He peered down the escarpment to the dark camp. There stood the scattered tents of the clans, beneath the little mesa on which their chief's tent rested. Andrah gazed down at them, remembering how they had chosen him allied leader after his father's death. He had had to best Khoramor Shant in the Three Trials, no mean feat considering the arcane powers of Shant's sister. Then Shant had challenged, and had desisted only at the urging of Starinor Zerdah and Molderan Kishen – although Kishen, too, questioned the leadership of the young Doralan.

But unity was necessary at least for the time. Thran of Eth, warlord of Mor, had murdered Mor's King Neren. To be certain of his security, Thran had then proceeded to a bloody pogrom, wiping out most of Neren's clan, the Solanans. The other clans of Elgain refused to swear allegiance, much less fealty, to the new ruler in Mor. Thran promised to bend their knees with fire and sword – and sent for mercenaries from his own land of Eth. At once, the secret meeting of the Elgain clans was called. But on the night before, Andrah's father suffered his last attack of the Grof

Sickness, and the meeting became a lengthier one than planned. There was the funeral for the old warrior, and the flame dances before his bier. Daron would return him to Andor in a new body; he had not merited retirement with his god by dying a warrior's death. Then came the business of Andrah's official ascension; eschewing pageantry, he had merely assumed his father's cloak and chair, shield and ax. Still plans could not be made to move against Thran before his foreign troops arrived. First there was the matter of choosing the leader of the temporary alliance against him.

Kishen of Molderan claimed the post, by right of age and family; his was the oldest clan in all Elgain and perhaps the world. So did young Shant of Khoramor claim the high honor, and all knew he was backed by his sister with her Starpowers. Starinor Zerdah nominated Andrah, and persuaded Kishen to join him in backing the son of the man they had acknowledged leader. And so Shant challenged.

The Three Trials; the challenge; its withdrawal, in a hot moment of hands on hilts. Then Doralan Andrah had swung his father's mantle about him and ascended to the chair and accepted, one by one, the patches of the other clans from the hands of their chieftains – even Shant's. And at last the planning began. They had begun to gather here, in the Mountains of Mist above Mor, as slowly as they dared in order not to arouse Thran's suspicion or attract his attention – now directed in the main to wenching, and elevating Ethites to powerful posts in Mor. And then the new clansleader, a mightily thewed man in his mid-twenties, had been struck down, seemingly by the same Grof Sickness that had always plagued – and finally killed – his father.

Now the body of Doralan Andrah stood looking down at the many tents of the allied clans. But Doralan Andrah was dying, perhaps dead, and within his big warrior's body was the Earthman Robert Cleve, who had answered an advertisement promising high adventure, excitement, danger, and challenge.

The danger and the excitement, he thought, *begin at once!* He smiled. High adventure, indeed! A foreign ruler to overthrow, before his foreign troops arrived to make the task harder or impossible. A witch's ensorcelments to avoid, and, Gordon had assured him, to fear. For on Andor, sorcery was real, not myth and fairy tale and priest talk. Two men wanted the power he held. And he in a body weakened by eleven days abed!

Flapping, the black cloak furled about him in the pale light of three of Andor's moons. His leather harness and abbreviated kilt gleamed in that same silvery light. The sword called 'bhur' hung heavy at his side. He stood, waiting for the approach of the other leaders who called him leader. And Robert Cleve smiled.

Chapter Two

The Clans of Elgain

'We are agreed, then,' Doralan said. 'We attack tomorrow and a day, from within. Stek, send riders down to the city at dawn, to prepare our allies and the clans-kin inside. We – Grof Starinor?'

The Starinor of Starinor rose, throwing back his cloak to show his fellow chieftains that he'd come armed to this moonlight meeting before the Doralan tent. His bristly gray mane seemed silver in the moonlight; his darker beard jutted from his warrior's chin. Deep-set eyes blazed about at his peers from beneath heavy brows.

'Pai, I came here sword-girt, beneath my cloak. Now we have agreed – and right calmly, too, as befits warrior chiefs – to mount our attack two days hence, I rise to tell you why. Perhaps it would be more politic to refrain. We have here acknowledged once more the leadership of the Doralan, and no treachery has marred our meeting. But never have I been known for my manners or for politic behavior. Here and now I accuse the Khoramor of Khoramor of plotting against our chief of chieftains, and of gaining the assistance of his Starpowered sister!' His arms, bare but for the copper brassard near his shoulder, swept out and extended to Khoramor Shant. Starinor Zerdah's ringless finger pointed.

'I make charge formally, in the presence of the clans, and name by demand here and now that Khoramor Shansi be brought here to answer in company with her brother.'

'Zerdah—'

Zerdah's eyes snapped to the speaker. 'Make no demurrers, Doralan Andrah! I speak in accord with our law, and demand group judgment. The Khoramor would undoubtedly fear your judgment to be prejudiced, because his would. I, too, fear the same, but in the opposite direction. You'd listen carefully and acquit them both, even if they confessed to a plot and my suspicion: that Khoramor Shansi sent upon you, by her Starpower, the sickness that has laid you low.' He turned back to the others. 'A sickness, my lords, that I have fought with all the power I could muster: that of my cousin, Witch of Starinor! Since the moment Andrah fell ill. I have had her hard at work in weaving spells to counteract the evil in his body – or mind, since no sign was found upon him but since he suffered from fever and delirium.'

Zerdah's big, gnarled hand, minus its third finger, lay curled loosely about the pommel of his sword. His eyes swept them all, including Andrah. Then they returned to stare implacably, malignantly at the young Khoramor.

Shant, Khoramor of Khoramor, was on his feet. Hurling back his purple cloak, he spread wide his arms. He wore an ungirt sleep tunic of white homespun.

'Not afflicted with the suspicious mind of the Starinor of Starinor, and with no such malice in my heart as his tongue seeks to place there, I show that I came unarmed and unarmored.' His hands clutched at the slanted closure of the tunic, jerked it open so that it flapped loosely about him. Beneath, his strong body was naked. He turned, again extending his arms, showing them all he spoke truth. Then he spoke on:

'I acknowledge the legality of the Starinor's accusation, but not its truth. It is wholly false. It is little more than I might expect, I admit, from a warrior forced to defend his keep against marauders. But that, Starinor Zerdah, was ten years past. Cannot your mind accustom itself to peace and trust of your peers? It was not one of us that attacked you in Starinor Keep, but the men from eastern Valnyra, starved from crop failure.' Chant swung to Andrah. 'I challenge you, Andrah. I have deferred that challenge until after we have won, in concert, over Thran. But . . . I have not "plotted against you." Nor has my sister, within my knowledge, sent spells upon you. She offered to fight for your life! I hail your miraculous recovery from what we all assumed was the Grof Sickness that killed your father in bed, that mighty Daron might have to send him back thus in a new body and a new life, seeking again his warrior's death.'

'Swear,' Molderan Kishen said quietly, in a voice like the crackling leaves of autumn. And Zerdah nodded, chewing at his fierce moustache.

Shant dropped one hand to where his bhur hilt would have been at his left hip; his right he raised to cover the patch of Khoramor on his left shoulder. 'In the presence of my peers, in the eyes of Daron and in fear of His anger, and on the patch and honor of all generations of Khoramor, I swear.'

Andrah glanced at Zerdah. Zerdah was still glowering at Shant.

'You swear what, Khoramor?'

Shant lifted his chin without looking at Zerdah. 'I swear that I have made no plots against the life of Grof Doralan Andrah, nor – to my knowledge – has my sister, Shansi.'

Andrah nodded. 'I am satisfied.'

Kishen nodded his white-fringed, balding head. 'I am satisfied.'

'I am satisfied,' Starinor Zerdah said, 'that I wrongly accused the Khoramor of Khoramor, and I make open apology and bow my head to challenge and invective.'

'I forego challenge and invective and accept the Starinor's apology, nobly put,' Shant said.

Andrah sighed and passed a finger across his brow with a little smile. 'Good, then. Now, my lords—'

'But I am not satisfied of the innocence of the witch Shansi.' Zerdah's deep voice broke in, as if he'd never ceased speaking. His thumbs were hooked into his copper-bossed swordbelt. 'My lord Khoramor has acquitted himself; no one knows of a grof who has foresworn himself since the days of the sixth clan' – he spat – 'a century ago. But I accused Khoramor Shansi, and I demand her presence here, and I do not retract.'

'Well spoke.'

The soft voice came from the darkness. Eyes swiveled and heads jerked. She came upon them then, swathed in a purple cloak bearing the Khoramor patch, a cloth-of-gold shield with two broken arrows, purple. Her eyes were the golden green of the lors that roamed these same mountain heights, descending at times to stare fire and hate out of the darkness at the world of men. Her hair was the deep red-brown of mahogany, though only Andrah thought so; only Robert Cleve had seen mahogany. Her brow was wide and high and pale, her cheeks gaunt beneath prominent bones, her nose thin and straight as a sword blade. Her mouth was wide, thin-lipped, and pink. Her features, Robert Cleve thought, were not beautiful, none of them. Yet she was more than pretty, this so-slender girl with the back-drawn mahogany hair and the wide mouth. All of her features, and, he was certain, even all her body, were she to appear nude, were as if in shadow; it was her eyes that drew a man's attention, clouded his mind, brought a frown to his brow.

'Well spoke,' the woman in the purple cloak said again, and walked among them as if she, too, were a grof. 'I need tell you none that I am Khoramor Shansi. I need remind you none that a woman's word is as naught, and that my swearing is meaningless in your eyes. Nevertheless' – the golden-green eyes seemed to flicker as they gazed into Andrah's own gray eyes, pale and lifeless by comparison – 'nevertheless, I swear to you, Andrah of Doralan, Grof of Elgain Grofts, that I have spoken no words, burned no candles, looked into no fires, consulted no wine-marc concerning you. Nor have I sent or attempted to send spells against you.'

She stepped to her brother's side and placed her left hand on his heart, while her right covered the patch of Khoramor on her cloak. 'This I swear in the presence of my lords, in the eyes of Daron and in peril of His anger, and on the patch and honor of all generations of Khoramor.' She hestitated a moment, then added, 'And on my brother's life.'

They all gasped. Shant included. He stepped back a pace, staring at her. His hair contained less red, his eyes less gold, though there was green there, in their brown.

The Witch of Khoramor smiled. 'Surprised, my noble lords? Shocked? Even you, my brother?' She laughed softly, in her throat, her slender throat that Andrah could have broken with one squeeze of his left hand. 'I offer myself to whatever trial my lords suggest or demand. But – if you can wait until sunrise, you will see that I have not plotted or spelled. Well you know the power of a witch; well you know that if I have lied I have called down demon-death upon my own beloved brother, a death that will strike before dawn.'

She turned, purple cloak whispering, to face the tall Zerdah with his gray mane. For a moment she gazed at him, their eyes meeting.

'Can you, will you wait, my lord of Starinor?'

Zerdah nodded. 'I am satisfied. I wrongly accused the sister of the Khoramor, and I bow my head to invective.'

Her laughter bubbled up again from her throat, like a fast-running river chuckling over little rocks in a shallow bed. 'But not to ensorcelment?' she asked in her soft voice, and Doralan Andrah's nape pricked. He felt gooseflesh race up his arms, and his groin tightened.

Zerdah's head snapped up. He slapped hands to pommel and patch, in the gesture of swearing; it was also the ward sign against sorcery.

Again the gaunt-cheeked girl chuckled. 'Save your poor cousin from her labors this time, Starinor of Starinor,' she said. 'I shall not graem against you.' She turned, glancing at Andrah, and he saw that her eyes could be semi-concealed beneath magnificent long lashes that made him want to leap from the stone on which he sat and seize her with no thought save of his own pleasure.

'We have need of each other,' she told them, 'all of us. We must remain united. Together we can crush Thran and his Ethite lap pets.' A slender arm, unbejeweled and pale, leaped from within the cloak she held about her from within. She pointed down the hill and to the west, where Mor lay, just out of sight around a rocky spur. 'There is the enemy,' she said. 'There is him we all accuse. There is him against whom I spell. There is him against whom the Witch of Starinor should be weaving her sorcery, not wasting her time and power trying to protect Andrah from the Grof Sickness that marks him for greatness!' Her eyes returned to Andrah; again she veiled them. 'My apologies, lord. The birth name of the Doralan slipped from my woman's lips.'

And she smiled at him, and bowed her head, and turned, and went away again into the night. Her feet made no sound; her cloak whispered.

'My sister speaks truth,' Shant said.

'Your sister speaks truth,' Andrah said, rising to his feet. 'The day after tomorrow, my lords.'

They left him, returning down the declivity to their own tents among their own clansmen.

In the tent of Khoramor the young clan lord slept fitfully and restlessly, muttering and sheened with sweat. Nearby, his witch-sister Shansi did not sleep, all that night. She murmured, she swore quietly, she cajoled, she burned candle and watched flame and gestured and hurled droplets from her pierced finger into the flame, talking on and on, weaving a long and difficult graem: spell.

A shadow hovered in the tent with her, a nigh-formless and yet nearly formed wraith that swirled above the sleeping Shant, and Shansi's eyes were upon it. Just before sunrise the shadow swirled as if in anger, and then there was an Otherworld moan and it streamed from the tent. Through the camp it went, riding the fog, and somewhere a young clansman screamed as he died a sudden and terrible death. Panting, covered with perspiration, Shansi fell down into a sleep from which she could not be wakened for twenty hours. She had saved her brother from the demon-death to which she'd doomed him.

Chapter Three

The Throne of Mor

The market of Mor seemed suddenly to go insane. There was little warning. One moment the scene was perfectly normal; the noisy, color-splashed crowd that daily made a beehive appear, drab, aimless, otiose by comparison. Then someone – no one was ever sure who – yelled at someone else. Why, no one was certain. A fine example of Kiran pottery got itself broken into several-score pieces. Someone else howled, and a beautifully cured ham arced through the air to fall into a trio of matrons who looked as though their spouses possessed wealth too large, and authority – perhaps whips – too small. Someone knocked someone else flailing backward into a bright yellow-and-red-and-royal-blue bazaar. Stall, poles, and awning came down with a terrific crash. A jonquil-robed man dodged desperately away – and smashed into a beautifully executed pyramid of glazed urns. Not one survived. People began screaming; many, at once.

The market appeared suddenly to go insane. Shrieks and jeers, threats and counterthreats rose mingling with ever-bluer invective to sunder the air. Everyone seemed to be shouting at once in a diaphanous cacophony of ear-menacing sound. And then everyone seemed to be fighting. Crockery and fruits, pots and vegetables, vases and cuts of meat, plain and fancy, whirled through the air in an endless stream.

A helmeted guardsman, one of Thran's Ethite imports, jerked apart two screeching women, managing to rip the dress of the more bosomy one. She screamed and shrank back, essaying – futilely – to cover her abundance with her hands. The other woman swung a wild blow at the guardsman; it failed to land as he backed a pace. Suddenly concerned, he put out a hand for the billhook he'd left leaning against the stucco wall. It was not there.

And the picaresque aspect of the scene came to a sudden end.

Before the guardsman could turn in search of his billhook, it burst into his back and passed through his body, to emerge dark-stained from his belly.

Across the agora two other guardsmen, Thran's men in their resplendent, cranberry-and-silver tunics, cracked a cursing merchant's skull and shoved his wife violently. She staggered whimpering back into the nearby stall of a silversmith. A moment later she emerged from the clattering wreckage swinging an ornate candlestick such as could be afforded only by wealthier nobles. It jellied the face of one guard; the other ran her through. As he yanked his sword free of her twitching body, a running man snatched up the first guard's halberd. With it he skewered the second soldier.

Word spread fast: Riot! Through the streets of Mor hurried the City Watch, a uniformed police force. They entered the central marketplace with lowered heads and leveled pikes. Behind them came militiamen, peering over the tops of their green-and-yellow shields.

Word spread fast: Throughout the walled city all knew of the riot in the marketplace.

The organized force that took the barracks of the City Watch was hardly noticed; all of them had covered or left elsewhere their Clan Doralan patches. Now other groups of uniformed men came a-running as smoke billowed from the barracks, black and thick and fearsome.

Within an hour of that first shout in the marketplace, the city on Sky River resembled nothing more than a gigantic madhouse.

Orders were issued and reissued; Watchmen and militia were dispatched to one quarter, only to be recalled to somewhere else. A detachment of men in the red-leather harness of Thran's archers trotted through the noisy streets to the tall gates facing the towering Mountains of Mist. They clanked and rattled to the gate, unshouldering their bows and shouting to the gate sentries; these trod a platform four feet below the top of the wall.

It was then that the clans attacked. They streamed out of the mountains like a rolling tidal wave of steel.

One of the gatemen shouted, pointing at the charging mass of warriors. Then he jerked, stiffened, and fell forward against the wall. He bounced back to fall backward onto the ground, driving deeper the arrow between his shoulder blades. The other gatemen fell, too, as the Doralans in the red-leather harness loosed their shafts.

Then they opened the gates. The clansmen rushed in. Above their helmeted heads bobbed the bright pennons of Molderan, of Starinor, of Khoramor, of Doralan, of Solanan.

Gradually the marketplace emptied of all but now-confused Watchmen and soldiery. The people vanished, leaving behind dead and dying and injured, amid the wreckage of the brightly colored stalls.

In the mouths of the dozen streets leading into the agora appeared warriors with naked swords; black-patched Doralans, and Khoramors with their gold-and-purple patches; black-helmed Starinors wearing silver patches shaped like four-pointed stars; the russet-clad archers of Clan Molderan, their harnesses jingling. What followed then was little less than a massacre.

'Up, men, follow me to the market!' an Ethite commander bawled, and his adjutant spitted him as one gaffs a fish.

'Up, men, follow me to the palace!' the adjutant bawled. 'Down with Thran the usurper!'

The defending followers of Thran soon found that most of the citizenry of Mor was against them – and those not, were not taking sides at all.

Soon Doralan Andrah was trading parries and ringing blows with two of the inner palace guardsmen. He bloodied his blade in the belly of one and grinned at the other. Abruptly the bedlam hushed. Andrah took a pace back and looked past his opponent; the man turned cautiously to follow his gaze.

Crimson-robed, crowned with the six-pointed chaplet of Elgain, Thran of Eth, formerly warlord and now King of Mor by virtue of having murdered his predecessor, stood tall and straight at the top of the six steps to his dais. His eyes stared down at the arrow quivering in his chest. Then his mouth bubbled scarlet and he leaned like a hewn tree. He tumbled down the dais steps. A Starinor warrior leaped forward. His saw-edged sword glittered in a descending arc of deadly steel. It rang from the floor, and from its edge sparks flew – and the bright crimson gush of the juice of Thran's life. His staring head rolled away from his body like a grotesque red-and-white ball.

The man facing Andrah of Doralan dropped his bhur with a clang and a clatter. The thud of his knee to the floor followed close after.

'Corpses, captives, or loyal followers, Doralan! Whichever you choose for us to be!'

'Up,' Doralan Andrah said, and strode past him. Up the gleaming floor of cream-colored tiles he strode, a fighting man in naught but boots and baldric, his loins covered by the short leather kilt that left bare his right thigh. There was blood on his bhur, and on the arm that wielded it, and on his leg, and splashed upon his black-and-silver shield. He tossed off his dented helm with its blue-black lor horns, sending it clattering to the floor. Ahead lay Thran's headless body, and beyond that, the six steps and the dais, and beyond that, the tall blood-wood throne of Mor with its silver chasing.

A dozen paces away he halted, his gray eyes fixed on the other man whose steps carried him toward the same destination. Khoramor Shant stared back. Both men's knuckles whitened about the tear drop hilts of their red-smeared swords. The gray eyes of Doralan gazed into the green-flecked ones of Khoramor.

'Doralan!'

The half-crouching clan chieftains turned at the shouted cry. It was Starinor Zerdah, smiling, his saw-toothed sword raised high. 'Doralan!' he bawled again.

'Doralan!' another voice shouted, and eyes rolled to Molderan Kishen. 'Pai! I, the Molderan or Molderan, eldest clan of Elgain, say again: Doralan! He who led us hence, he whose planning brought us to Mor and our high throne with the loss of so few lives – and with Mor's walls intact. Doralan, worthy successor to his father, worthy successor to King Neren!'

And they took up the shout, the others crowding the throne room, and Doralan Andrah ascended the steps to the tall, hard chair. He turned and stood there a moment, gazing down at them. Then he sat. Doralan Andrah, Robert Cleve, the first Earthman on Andor, was Grof of Grofs, King of Mor and Elgain, and thus Morgrof of Elgain.

Chapter Four

The Morgrof of Elgain

Ledni of Starinor shook her head with its tight brown curls.

'No, Doralan,' she said, for witches call no man king; indeed, none of the families called the new Morgrof of Elgain aught else but Doralan. He was the Doralan of Doralan; what higher title was there? They'd elected him chief of chiefs, Grof of Grofs, Doralan Andrah did not, however, rule them. They remained his peers, they and the curly-headed cousin of Starinor Zerdah: Ledni, Witch of Starinor.

'No, Doralan,' she repeated, 'it was not my doing, nor any other's save yours and that of the Morgrof of Eth. 'Twas he honored the old agreement and called back the Ethites sent for by Thran. Under pain of attack by his own army, he recalled them, and back they went all, grumbling. Mor is safe, Doralan. Elgain is safe.' Her eyes darkened and her head bent, the round head with its curly mop so unlike what one might expect in a Starpowered One.

'But ye, Doralan, you're only as safe as ye keep yourself. Powerful spells I've wove about ye. But spears and arrows, pai, and even swords – these move faster than protecting spells and the forces they call forth.' She glanced about, round-faced, rosy-cheeked, a girl of less than twenty years with bright eyes beneath perennially touseled hair. Her snubbed nose was tiny above a puckered little mouth shaped like the short bow of a mountain herder. And she was Starpowered, and of Starinor, oldest of families. Down to her had come centuries of generations of Andorite witchery. Now she'd taken on her square little shoulders the protection of the new Morgrof of Elgain.

'I can protect myself against bhurs, Ledni, and spears and arrows too,' the bare-chested young king said.

'So ye can. But ye've no power, Doralan Andrah, against the powers given some few by the twinkling stars themselves.

I have, for I have the power in me from my grandmother and my mother before me. Not in the Starinor ring I wear, nor in this four-pointed bauble so cold, always so cold with its starfire, between my breasts. It's in here,' she said, touching her heart beneath a tiny round hillock, 'and here. Pai, mostly here.' And she tapped her curl-straggled forehead. 'Listen to me!'

'Why listen, Ledni? It's I to my business and you to yours. I'll thank you, and put matters dark and sorcerous out of my head.'

Her black eyes flashed and her bosom heaved as she bent fierily toward him. Her fingertip touched his bare chest without regard for his rank or care for his sex. She tapped, once, twice, three times, just beside the broad, padded baldric he wore, even lounging on his couch of dark velvet.

'Put them from your mind, indeed! More fool you, Doralan Andrah! No, shy not away, and don't bother to pretend anger or act kingly with me, Andrah of Doralan Keep! Look here. Listen close, and in Daron's name take heed: Place no trust in the sister of the Khoramor!'

'Ledni—'

'Hush a moment, Ando,' she said, using the name he'd heard from no one save his father for many years; not even Biyah dared use the childhood diminutive. 'Hush I say, and listen.'

He uncrossed a bare leg and swung it down to the floor, bending toward her. He touched his fingers to her lips.

'No, witchgirl, you listen. We've dissolved our quarrel and made our peace, Shant and I, and Shansi and I. Shant acknowledges me morgrof. And his enchantress-sister – why, she's his *sister*! We've become friends, these past fifteen days since we retook Mor. Shant wishes me no ill, and Shansi is subject to him.'

Slowly, Ledni's little mouth rounded into a shocked O. Her eyes were wide and incredulous as she stared at him. She rose slowly without taking her gaze from his face, a short, plumpish girl in a carelessly sewn, carelessly chosen tunic of medium brown that was too long to flatter her thighs and too short to enhance her knees. It rippled, the tunic whose shade could flatter no woman, as she trembled.

'Oh, Andrah! Why must a warrior so strong in the thews be so weak in the head! He *hates* you, Andrah, he seethes and bubbles and boils with it! Oh, if I could lend you my power, my feelings for but a moment! Then you could know what I feel from him, radiating from him like heat from a torturer's brazier! He wants the power they voted to you, Andrah, and he wants more. He wants your life, he wants you on your *knees*, Andrah. And you must understand that it isn't Shansi who is subject to him. She is the strength of Khoramor, Andrah; it's she should have been the male! But she is a woman, and her only hope for the power she wants is through her brother. He wants the clanpatches you hold, and she wants him to have them – so that she herself will possess more power.'

Andrah first smiled, then laughed. He bent to pluck a cluster of blue grapes from a green-glazed bowl.

Her face twisting, Ledni slapped it from him. Grapes plopped and rolled as the bowl crashed to the floor. He jerked his face up angrily, big fists clenching. Then he saw the hot tears in her eyes, glistening on her cheeks, and he frowned. Slowly his hands relaxed, opened. And Ledni hurled herself against his breast, her arms about him. She squeezed him to her, and he felt her tears on his chest.

'Oh, Ando! Why won't you see! Why won't you protect yourself! Take the love at hand – and the protection. I'll watch over you always, I'll—'

And then she released him and drew back quickly, embarrassedly, a boyish girl with a boyish figure and curly, unruly hair.

'Make me one promise, Doralan of Doralan. Make me one promise, I beg you. On your patch.'

Frowning a little, he nodded. He laid hand to hip where his sword would be, wore he one, and with his other palm he covered the Doralan clanpatch on his chest strap. He nodded again. 'By the patch of Doralan, I promise.'

'Give to Shansi, Witch of Khoramor,' she said, eyes and voice intense, 'nothing of yourself. Do you understand? *Give her nothing of yourself.* Not a drop of blood, not a fingernail paring or a hair from your head, not a drop of sweat from your body. With that precaution, perhaps I can protect you. Promise, Andrah.'

He promised, and she nodded and gazed at him a long moment with soft, troubled eyes, and then she turned and left him. She ran, ran boyishly and in a manner ill-befitting a witch and a Starinor and the cousin of the Starinor of Starinor.

And in another place:

The fire flickered and danced, casting a fleeting, eerie glow of gold and crimson on the features of the thin-faced woman staring into the flames. Her eyes returned its glow, flashing golden green like the eyes of the lors that roamed the upper Mountains of Mist. In the wraithlike witchfire she watched Starinor Ledni extract her promise and flee the draped room, watched Doralan Andrah gaze after the awkwardly running girl, saw him shake his head and bend to pick up a grape.

From the bowl by her naked right hip Khoramor Shansi drew a pinch of herbs; from the bowl on her left she scooped a handful of strange vermilion dust. Her lips moved as she raised her arms, then threw herbs and dust into the flames. The fire sprang up with a whooshing sound. Orange smoke boiled and writhed, seemingly striving to assume some shape it could not quite manage. Shansi's eyes gleamed and emitted a xanthic glow while she watched the amorphous twisting of the smoke, the lips of her wide mouth moving, moving.

On the eighteenth day after his ascension to the unpadded throne of Mor, Doralan Andrah was presented with a strange gift.

'Burn it, my noble lord,' the Witch of Khoramor said, as he peered into the black bowl she held out to him, cradled between her two hands. 'You must not be so careless, I cannot always be on the watch.'

He frowned, pinching from the bowl its contents readily visible against the black, baked clay; a single fingernail paring. Holding it betwixt thumb and forefinger, he looked questioningly at her.

She lowered her head. The bodice of her chrysoprase gown was loose, and low, and it gaped when she bent forward, standing on the third step to his dais. She seemed unaware of the display she made of herself as she watched him from beneath those long, dark lashes.

'Burn it,' she repeated in her throaty voice, 'or eat it, Doralan of Doralan.'

Mechanically he nodded, closing his palm on it. 'Thank you, Shansi.'

'Anything,' she said, and her voice was soft. Hair the color of bloodwood swished forward to caress his knee as she inclined her head. And she backed down the steps, still bowing. He watched the sinuous sway of her slender hips beneath the straight gown as she left the hall, her feet scarce seeming to touch the floor. He watched, and his temples throbbed.

On the second-and-twentieth day of his reign, the Morgrof of Elgain sat in the verdant garden behind his palace. He was surrounded by blossoms of many shapes and colors and sizes – heliotrope and henna and cerulean and butter yellow – and by trees that towered six times the length of his body before sprouting broad-sweeping branches heavy with mauve fruits amid emerald leaves thick as hair on a man's head. Peridot ferns with leaves like a ball gown's fringed border nodded and stirred in the ghost of a breeze, whispering their secrets as they caressed one another. Biyah had left him, hustling the barber who'd begged to loosen my lord's warrior's knot and curl his straight-growing hair, since now he wore the scarlet robe.

He heard the rustle in the saffron ferns growing close to his bench, and the morgrof laid hand to dagger hilt.

Her voice was soft and throaty as always: 'Not necessary, my lord. No enemy approaches, though I offer apology for coming so quietly I aroused your warrior instinct. It is good to know that the Morgrof of Elgain possesses a warrior's ears and reflexes.'

She swayed into his sight, reed-slim and intensely desirable in a soft-draped gown of palest green that clung to her slenderness as if aware of its enviable task. Her lips quirked slightly in her little hint of a smile. Then her eyes dropped to his feet and widened, and she gasped before she bent swiftly. Again he saw that the low round neck of her gown was loose, and that she was warm and alive and whitely bare within it. His throat went dry and he willed his eyes elsewhere, but they were as if entranced.

On one knee at his feet, Shansi plucked an invisible something from among the olive blades of grass and held it before her eyes. She extended it to him, and he saw that her nails were long and precisely the color of her hair.

'Oh my *lord*! A hair from your head – please! I beg of you, be more careful. If you are sure of Biyah, be certain he catches and collects and burns all such as this. Here.'

He opened his palm and waited, watching her fingers move gently. Then he saw it, a black hair from the recent trimming of his head, lying on his palm. Frowning, gazing into the golden green of her eyes, he closed his hand upon it. She gazed up at him with an expression of great concern, remaining on her knees.

'He did well, my lord,' she said at last. 'You are more handsome than ever.'

And she laid a hand on his bare knee to assist her in swaying lithely to her feet. He reached for the soft, cool hand with its long fingers, but he touched only his own knee as she withdrew and moved away, the pale-green gown clinging and caressing. Andrah watched, clenching his fist about the forgotten hair. Unusually, he called for wine.

The pipes wailed and tootled, wailing and keening in the banquet hall of the palace of the city called High; Mor. Tambours rattled, dainty ankle bells tinkled, muffled tympani rumbled and throbbed. The girl who danced was perhaps sixteen, the product of constant training as a dancing girl since her birth in far Shivshor. Thin earrings of great diameter danced and sparkled as she moved, just brushing her bare shoulders. Her hair was a rippling cascade of blue-black down her back to her tiny round rump. Silver bells gleamed and tinkled from her wrists and ankles as her bare feet became a coppery blur in the ever-increasing tempo of her dance. She wore but precious little, and that diaphanous and flesh-colored, high-cut and low-slung.

Stek, a giant warrior of Clan Doralan, grasped a passing maidslave and drew her down to him, the contents of her fruit bowl and of her halter spilling all over him. Her giggle was drowned by his deep-throated laughter. Farther down the great hall, wearing blue so dark it was nearly black, the Witch of Starinor lounged on a divan beside her cousin Zerdah. His larger couch was occupied by both himself and the blond slave who fed him azure grapes, one by one, from her azure lips. The Starinor saw no one; his witch-cousin Ledni saw only the muscular young lord at the head of the room.

Across from her, ignoring her lordly brother's constant ringing of the ankle bells of the girl on his couch, the Witch of Khoramor watched Starinor Ledni watching Doralan Andrah. A tiny smile tugged at Shansi's wide mouth.

And the Morgrof of Elgain watched her.

A girl twining sinuously at his feet caressed his ankle with soft hands. After a time he glanced down at her with a little frown. She lay half on her back, displaying most of her white self in a mulberry-colored gown cut low at the bodice and high on the thigh. She smiled up at him.

'You see neither the dancer nor me, my lord,' she said in a calculatedly husky voice. 'Both of us should be enraged. Instead, we are desolated.'

'Who could overlook either of you, Losane?' Andrah said, bending a little to stroke her hair.

She thrust out her lower lip and rolled her eyes beneath their purple-painted lids. 'Ah, mere chivalry, my lord, and transparent, too! Ye've eyes for none but that thin Witch of Khoramor! Does she indeed possess hips and bosom, one wonders?' And Losane displayed her own with justifiable pride. No second glance was necessary to prove their presence.

'I – I was watching her brother's game,' Andrah began weakly, and the girl at his feet chuckled.

'Oh, my lord! What of our land when the morgrof will not speak true even to a pleasuremaiden! Tsk!' She pursed her lips prettily; they were dyed to match her eyelids. 'Never have I understood my betters. My lord sits there, watching her . . . she is at the far end of the room . . . and watching you!'

'Oh, she's not—' But as Andrah looked, he caught Shansi jerking her head away. His arms tingled and he felt suddenly overwarm; she *had* been watching him, furtively, while he looked elsewhere!

The couchgirl chuckled again. 'Eh? Eh, my lord?' She shook her sleek head. 'The nobility! Were ye of less birth, either of ye, ye'd already have left this noisy place to tryst somewhere darker and more quiet! Why, my lord – ye seem surprised. Is it possible the morgrof knows not what we all know? – that the Khoramor Shansi is struck to the heart with you, and hardly able to keep her eyes from your face or your name from her lips? Why, 'tis only her pride and station, my lord, and the recent trouble betwixt yourself and her brother – these are all that keep her from laying herself at your feet!'

Andrah gazed down at the girl. Slowly he raised his head to stare down the hall at Shansi. Absently, he reached for his goblet. Smiling, the pleasuremaiden Losane guided the cup into his hand, noting the tremble of his fingers.

Later, while the Morgrof of Elgain lay alone on his pallet, gazing at the ceiling of his huge – and lonely – bedchamber, the couchgirl Losane smiled again as the so-slender woman in the hooded, unmarked cloak clinked one, two, three silver stolars into her palm.

Chapter Five

The Witch of Khoramor

The planets move; the suns move; the galaxies move. The universe moves, its origin unknown, its destination unfathomable. Whence came it and its galaxies and suns and planets and satellites? Where go they, on their constant journey through space inconceivably vast?

Where have they been, the countless planets revolving about the countless suns in the – countless? – galaxies in the universe – universes?

Perhaps Daron, or God, or Allah, or Yahweh – perhaps He knows. Perhaps.

The Earth, Gordon had told Robert Cleve on Earth, had passed with its neighbors once and perhaps more than once through an enigmatical zone. A zone in which the laws of cause and effect were suspended; in which that which could be dreamed might happen, in which Aristotelian logic – A is A – did not hold immutable and unchallenged sway. A zone in which nothing was *necessarily* true; nothing *necessarily* followed. During that time locusts fell from the sky like rain, and wooden staffs become writhing serpents, and the Nile ran red. During that time a bush burned, but was not burned, and perhaps a voice issued from it. During that time the Reed Sea was parted or stricken arid, and the folk hero Moses led his fleeing followers across. There was magic in the world, and spells, and divination and conjuration: miracles. Magic and sorcery, witches and warlocks and magi and diviners had existed on Earth. Perhaps more than once.

Then the Earth and its neighbors had passed on, moving on in their interminable journey, and again there had been Natural Law.

Sorcery existed now, Gordon told Robert Cleve, on the far, far planet its inhabitants called Andor. Witches cast their spells – graems – and the spells took effect. Fire revealed answers and pictures. Smoke congealed, took palpable forms. Words became incantations, and incantations became conjuries, and conjuries became fact.

There were enchantresses on Andor, Gordon told Cleve. Sorcerers and sorcery. And they ensorceled. Believe, Gordon told Cleve, and fear them. If you find a witch against you, beware her. If a witch befriends you, accept her friendship willingly and gratefully. Cultivate her. Only witches can fight witches, Gordon told him, with certainty of success.

Robert Cleve was forced to believe that there was a world called Andor, that there lived a man named Doralan Andrah. And that the nameless organization on Earth, with which the bespectacled man called Gordon was his only contact, was in contact, too, with Andor. He was forced to believe that the brain of a man from Earth could be transferred across the airless parsecs to Andor – and retain the Andorite's memories.

These things he was forced to believe, because he was here, on Andor, and he was Robert Cleve – and Doralan Andrah.

Doralan Andrah believed in witches, and the Otherworld, and enchantment and the Starpowered Ones and their graems. And so believed all his fellows.

But Robert Cleve was of Earth. Worse, he was of America, where belief in magic is laughed at and sneered at, save only in church and on Wall Street. Despite all Gordon had said, despite all he had seen and heard here, despite the beliefs of his peers and of the memories he now possessed, Doralan Andrah's memories, Cleve found it most difficult to accept witches and witchery. Certainly, miracles were possible – all that was needed was belief and a project not too impossible. With belief, one could be cured of nearly anything, achieve anything. But . . . spells? Fire and candle and blood, fingernails and hairs and darkly murmured words, waving hands and wraithy creatures from some shadowy Otherworld?

No, this was too much.

Thus he believed that Ledni believed in her power, his childhood friend, tomboyish Starinor Ledni. And Shansi? He was not so certain about Khoramor Shansi. She was, he was sure, a very intelligent woman in her early twenties –

and his Earth-American mind told him that no intelligent person could truly believe in the things of which Grimm and Andersen had written.

She was fascinating, a word that appears among the synonyms for sorcerous. She would not leave his thoughts, she and those strange, jungle-cat eyes, the rich mahogany hair, the high cheekbones above model-gaunt cheeks; that wide, thin-lipped mouth that seemed to beckon his kisses, promising to flower beneath his lips. The lissome body, so slim and yet so graceful, so womanly with its svelte, swaying hips and flowing walk – that, too, beckoned, with a call more ancient than any monument on Andor or on Earth. There was a tightness in his flat belly, a dryness in his throat, a throb at his temples, an ache in his thighs. When she was not present his eyes searched for her. When she was, he strove to keep his gaze from her, fighting himself. And he lost battle after battle.

The thought never occurred to him that there was a word on Earth for the mental-physical attraction he felt; a word in songs and books and poems.

Bewitched.

So it was that Ledni of Starinor wept and loved and spelled her spells; and hoped, and murmured, and watched, ever she watched. In despair. In vain. But with hope yet: Shansi possessed things of him, but she possessed nothing of himself that he had given her.

Nevertheless Ledni strove in vain.

For it happened, somehow, that the night was dark and redolent of a thousand natural perfumes, that the room was darkened and beautiful with draperies and carven panels, and alive with the mingled scents of many flowers and incense and a perfume of necromantic creation and enchanting power. And he was there, and she was there: Doralan Andrah, Morgrof of Elgain, and Shansi, enchantress of Clan Khoramor. The gown she wore was a clinging carass of wispy aquamarine on her slenderness. Her hair was loose, a pearl-strewn, sheening mass about her pale shoulders and pale face with its golden-green eyes. The wine was unwatered, the divan too near, her svelte hips and silken-clad thighs irresistible.

Then his harness and red robe and her gown were forlorn together on the floor, and the candles burned low, flickering over the twining limbs on the pillow-strewn couch. She tasted his wand of masculine magic, and he delved deep into the arcane body of witchcraft. The candles burned still lower, and he slept. But Shansi slept not. Some strange dust from a concealed pocket pouch sparkled in the air above the candles, and their flame changed. He slept more deeply, alone on the couch, asleep, and his harness was now alone on the floor.

In the corridor without, the giant warrior Stek looked up as the paneled door opened softly. He gazed at her without friendliness, knowing only a part of what had occurred within his lord's apartment. And she gazed back with eyes of green and gold, smiling and murmuring, and soon Stek was asleep. She fled then, carefully, on feet that scarce touched the palace floors. She left the palace, walking carefully, guarding closely and carefully and delightedly the gift Andrah had given her, willingly; something of himself.

Soon she was naked again and seated cross-legged before her blue-writhing witchfire. She murmured, she gestured, weaving her graem.

And in another place:

Ledni, Witch of Starinor, started up gasping from her own fire, staring at the flame picture before her. Unheeded were her woman's tears at the kisses she'd seen; now her face bore a mask of horror. It was as a witch rather than as a woman that she cried:

'No! No, Ando! Don't! You're giving her—'

But he did, thoughtlessly, and she saw him fall into a sleep first natural and then enchanted by Shansi's power. She saw Shansi leave him there, guarding well the precious gift Doralan Andrah had given her of himself, transferring it from his body to hers. Then the fire darkened, and Ledni knew that Shansi's work had begun, for Ledni was unable to see into Shansi's keep.

Ledni swung a cloak about herself and fled into the night.

As the morgrof slept, as his giant guardian slept, so slept the palace, now, enveloped by a strange, clinging mist. In the innermost chamber of her very private keep within the city of Mor, the Witch of Khoramor sat cross-legged on the floor before her fire, naked and pale, for witches practice their craft not in peaked hats and black robes but with both mind and body open and unadorned. Into the flame she dashed the small sponge containing his gift. The fire hissed and whooshed and leaped high and poured smoke upward to the ceiling. It writhed, that smoke of virulent ensorcelment, thick and coppery, and it formed, slowly, coalescing as if shaped by the hands of an invisible sculptor. It swirled into legs, and arms, and a torso, and a head with a warrior's club of hair on its back.

Shansi looked up at the image.

'You are not of this place,' she whispered, for so she had learned, and her lips barely moved. 'You are not Doralan Andrah. Return . . . return . . .' Many times she repeated the word, but nothing happened: the specter would not depart. She frowned. 'Very well. If ye'll not return then, whence ye came, hear these words as ye sleep, and obey them: Become who you are, what you are. That and naught else. Forget all else save who ye truly be, in that other place and that other life. Doralan Andrah's mind and memories are not yours, thief . . . return them to him!'

And she clapped her hands, calling a name. The coppery smoke-image collapsed in upon itself and swirled and vanished, vanished without drifting away. New smoke crawled up the wall from the witchfire. It rose up and darkened, growing darker and darker until it was an unreflecting, impenetrable black. Again it formed, and this time red eyes stared at their invoker from its writhing depths, eyes that glowed and flashed and spoke pure malignance.

'Stek will remember nothing,' Shansi said, and the Otherworld eyes blinked; a headless nod. 'We will cast the black mantle of guilt over his shoulders. But these menace, and must be final – three who have aided me and must have ever-silent tongues, and one who is my deadliest enemy. These are their names: enasoL, and haruJ and hanroB and' – her lip twisted, her eyes glittered – 'and indeL! Go!'

Again the eyes blinked. The shadowy smoke-image flowed out the door, beneath it, and Shansi sat alone, waiting, smiling. Then she rose and called to two strong men who feared her power – and with just cause. Their names were Jurah and Bornah, and while they were on her orders they were safe from Otherworld powers.

The couchgirl Losane swept with her little smile from the privatemost chamber of the new Watch Commander of Mor, swinging her dark cloak about herself. Nestled against her soft belly as she hurried along the left bank of the river bisecting Mor – indeed, the city had grown up along first one, then the opposite bank of the River Sky – was the warming chill of good silver coin. She had it snuggled comfortingly to her, above her tight-drawn cincture. For swirled about her ankles and paled the moonslight as she hurried along Sky River's left bank.

She chuckled.

She had come far, from the squalor into which she had been born. Sold into slavery by her father that he and his wife might eat, she had been brought to Mor and, though ill-used, never beaten. Fortunately for her; for Daron, lover of beauty, had smiled upon her and given her the face and body he loved to look down upon. One of Thran's men had brought her to the palace, and her living standards had risen again. Then she had met the Starpowered Khoramor, and carried out her mission at the banquet, receiving three silver stolars from the Khoramor witch's own slim hand. With these she'd bought perfume still more costly, raiment still more diaphanous and thus more costly, spun by the red spiders of Rivshar, and jewelry more ladylike and eye-catching than her couchgirl's bells. Now she was in her own element, and well on her way to making knees bend. The Watch commander was a simple matter. And not ungenerous.

Next she would—

The fog seemed to thicken, to darken, to tighten about her. It pressed her body, clouded her eyes, cloyed her nostrils.

Suddenly she found that her feet would no longer move, nor could she raise her smoke-imprisoned hands to tear at the smoky cage about her head. She screamed, but the sound carried to no ears other than her own, and as she drew a deep breath she took in only the air she had expelled in the futile shriek. The fog had become dark smoke, tight about her as hostile arms. Her air grew more stale with each desperate breath. It was the fog, the smoke, become an impermeable cage, a shield about her, admitting no air and allowing no sound to escape.

The hopes of the couchgirl Losane fled with her beauty, as her eyes popped wide and wider and her tongue jabbed far out, quivering from her gaping mouth, seeking the air that was no longer there. The bosom with which Daron had been generous and with which Losane had been equally generous ceased to move. And then her life fled, her spirit journeying to Daron to be returned to Andor again in a body less lovely, and the shadow-thing swirled away on another mission as the couchgirl Losane slumped into Sky River with a muffled splash.

The Watch commander of Mor was stricken for days and unhappy for a week. Then he found another daughter of Daron eager for success, and he thought no more of Losane, ever.

In the corridor outside his lord's room Stek the Strong slid down the wall, tilted, and eased sideways onto the floor. His snoring was not disturbed by the passage of the two patchless men, both armed and cloaked, who entered the room of the sleeping Morgrof of Elgain. They were steering his naked, cloak-swathed form through the door when the Witch of Starinor, her dark eyes streaming tears that glistened on her face, stepped before them. Her Starinor-patched cloak swirled.

'I am Ledni, Witch of Starinor,' she said, in a sob-choked voice. 'Return him to his bed, on pain of demon-death!'

They blanched and nearly dropped their deep-sleeping burden. They backed, and then swung again toward Andrah's couch to return him to its rumpled fabrics. The little cry at the doorway made them look again at her, and their faces went still whiter.

She struggled in the writhing, tentacular grip of a great cloud of dark smoke. Her lips moved rapidly, summoning aid from its own world. It was not bravery moved the man holding Andrah's feet; the smoke-thing attacked Ledni of Starinor, and must thus emanate from his mistress Shansi; it did not want him, its ally. He moved swiftly. His dagger wheeped from its sheath to glitter a moment in the waning candlelight of Andrah's bedchamber. Then it swung down. Inches of icy steel slid into Ledni's body, just between the wide-set little apples of her bosom. The smokecloud swirled away as she sank down.

They left her there, lying half across the still-snoring Stek and bleeding on his huge calf. The man whose dagger it was, was no fool, else Shansi would not have recruited him. He bent and appropriated Stek's dagger, sheathing it at his own hip. Then he withdrew his smeary blade from the girl and slid it beneath Stek's hand.

They carried their cloak-muffled burden down to the river, there stretched it on the waiting raft, taking back the mantle so that the sleeping morgrof was nude. They stood on the bank, near the golden-eyed woman in the gently flapping purple cloak, watching as the Morgrof of Elgain floated away, through the city and from it, southward on the ever-widening Sky River, whose southern mouth none had ever seen.

They turned then to receive from their Starpowered employer their reward. She gave it not; they received it from the swirling black cloud-fingers of her demon, and she watched and waited until their bodies plop-plopped into the river to join Losane.

Alone with her knowledge, Shansi, Witch of Khoramor, turned and walked back to her fire. She had done much; she was exhausted; there remained yet much to do.

PART TWO

Robert Cleve

Chapter Six

The River of No Memory

Robert Cleve awoke. For a moment he lay still, staring up at darkness.

No, not darkness. A night sky, yes, but a sky alight with stars strewn like scintillant gems upon a jeweler's case of black velvet. A sky lit further by three baubles much larger than the others, one rather greenish, the others pale and silver-glowing. Robert Cleve's eyes rolled from one to the other.

The stars were totally unfamiliar, nor was there any pattern or conformation he recognized. The larger jewels were . . . moons.

Robert Cleve frowned. Robert Cleve? No. He was not Robert Cleve.

He was . . .

'My God! He did it! Gordon did it – but he failed! I'm not on Earth! But I do NOT have the memories he said I would have!'

For a few seconds his mind tried to panic. He fought back, silently, quelling the rising cloud that sought to unnerve him from within. He was on Andor. He'd been told he would be – Doralan Andrah. Oh yes, Doralan Andrah, and the first name was the last. That is, on Earth the name would be Andrah Doralan, and here his own name would be Cleve Robert. Doralan. A noble of some sort, a man with a mission and a future of importance . . . of some sort. Someplace. But he could not remember!

He had been told that he would possess all Doralan Andrah's memories.

But he possessed none.

He knew only the name, and the language he had been taught by hypnorem, instead of gaining it from Doralan's mind. A few other things: This was Andor, a perilous, primitive planet spinning close to a young sun, a planet on which barbaric strength and swordsmanship existed side by side with sorcery and witchcraft – if one could be expected to believe in such – and ferocious beasts, birds, even plants – and men.

Slowly he became aware of his surroundings. He had explored the inner situation, with little satisfaction. Now he turned to the outer.

He lay on his back on a wooden platform some seven feet long by about four feet wide. The gentle liquid sounds he heard, the constant lapping, the gentle undulance – these existed because the platform on which he lay outstretched was a raft. It – he – was moving, along a broad watercourse bordered by shadowy trees.

He was naked. Unclothed, unarmed, on a strange river, on a strange planet, beneath a strange sky with three moons.

He found himself laughing.

Well, he'd asked for it. He had wanted excitement, adventure, danger. He'd been promised all those, as well as the constant proximity and possibility – probability! – of sudden, horrible death.

He had to chuckle. Had he been tricked? Perhaps the bespectacled man named Gordon, the man with the nameless organization on Earth – perhaps he had tricked his recruit. And perhaps, that recruit thought, perhaps Gordon and his organization knew less than they thought or claimed. Or maybe the brown-suited man and his organization had merely erred.

'Well, he'd been promised precious little, Cleve thought. And he had received no more than he'd been promised!

Lying on his back, naked, floating helplessly downriver on the oarless raft, he gazed up at the alien sky. He firmed his lips. All right: he was here. Presumably he occupied the body of someone named Doralan Andrah. Presumably there had been a slip. This was not like setting forth in Africa in a Land Rover with an experienced, Aussie-accented guide and an assortment of gear and high-powered weapons. This was not like seeking the mighty tigers of India, armed with heavy guns and riding a heavy beast with leathery gray skin. Perhaps this was more dangerous than Vietnam, where a man's sole duty was to commit murder as many times as possible. At least there he had had training, weapons, companions – and a helmet.

Here he had nothing, yet he laughed. He had plenty. He had Doralan Andrah's body, a hard, iron-muscled body in fine condition. (Why? Had not Gordon said Andrah had lain long abed? Had there been a time lapse?) He had his brain, the fine brain of Robert Cleve of Earth. More: He had the determination, the mental strength, the total inability ever to quit, that were Robert Cleve's great assets. And the taciturnity and impetuousness that were perhaps assets, perhaps liabilities.

'I'll fight you, Andor,' he muttered. 'I'll fight you – and we'll see which of us is the stronger.'

And he laughed again, and the water gurgled and lapped, and he fell asleep.

Chapter Seven

The River of Death

Morning. Morning beneath a young sun, bloated and yellow-red. A young sun, not yet white or even fully yellow, but so close it radiated intense heat. It was too large, in a sky too purpled, as if painted by an artist who had mixed red pigment with his blue by accident and rushed on with his job anyhow. Squinting, Cleve rolled his head.

The river's gentle current held him in its center, so that the lavishly verdant shore was thirty feet away on either side. The water was strangely reddish, reflecting the sky. The shores were riotous, eye-searing, psychedelic with color. Huge ferns, tall as a man and taller, leaned their jonquil-yellow fronds out as if to admire their golden reflections in the vitriform surface of the water. Among them long-stemmed flowers nodded; sprawling, violet cup-shapes with yellow centers, like pasqueflowers – if Earthly pasqueflowers could somehow attain the size of dinner plates with hairy stems thick as a man's thumb. There were twining clusters with blossoms magenta and snowy; tendrilly vetchlike beauties that climbed the ferns and tree trunks in shapes resembling huge peas. Heavy-leafed, triple-sepaled blossoms with three veined petals resembled trilliums seen through a magnifying glass. He knew their names – plumenia, and thrileen, and meiane, and jalalis.

Above them reared tralib trees with bluish leaves and huge furry balls the size of Cleve's head. Aspenlike beauties were hung with trailing veils of something resembling Spanish moss – if Spanish moss were scarlet, and quivering as if alive. Behind them, deeper in the forest that bordered Sky River on both sides, reared sequioialike giants with their berylline heads scraping pink-bellied clouds. Birds trilled and warbled and skirled like bagpipes, and those latter orange-and-green-and-blue creatures of the sky were skreets, which could be taught to imitate speech.

Robert Cleve rolled onto his side, cautiously. He sat up with just as much care on his doorlike craft. He sat still, riding to he knew not where from he knew not whence. How far had he come, from wherever he'd come from?

He was still: thinking, assimilating.

He floated, naked.

The orange sun swung up overhead, hesitated, and then reluctantly began its descent. Cleve's belly grumbled its discontent, and he slapped it angrily. It was hard, muscularly divided into two hemispheres, each of which was divided and divided again by taut musculature. He flexed arms with mighty, knotted thews rolling beneath gleaming flesh like hand-burnished bronze. He raised one leg, noting that the naked thigh did not quiver, that the muscle leaped up in his calf like a ball of hard leather imbedded in a sheath of smooth flesh, deep bronze in color. It was a powerful body, a fighting body.

He floated.

The trees whispered, the insects chittered, the birds trilled and caroled and flitted and swooped. Sky River flowed on, and words entered his mind, words in a language now foreign:

'He don't say nothin' . . . He just keeps rollin' along . . .'

Peacefully, calmly, quietly, Ole Man Sky rolled along.

Until the peace and tranquillity was destroyed by yells and screams that sent the birds in terrified flapping protests.

Cleve nearly swamped his raft in his jerking about to look at the source of the noise. Men. Men with bronzed skin the color of his own, with hair uniformly black and shaggily page-boyed, mouths wide as they voiced their savage yells. They pointed, jabbering. They wore belts of poorly tanned hide, supporting long daggers, one on each hip. Each wore an armlet of some sort of long-haired, orangeish hide; tribal totem, he presumed. They wore nothing else, save for the paint on their lower bellies and thighs. And . . . Andor or not, surely Nature did not give men such teeth. They had been filed.

Not only were these swordless men savages, they were cannibals!

Two, either braver than their fellows or detailed by their big-bellied leader to fetch the naked, unarmed man from his precarious barge, leaped into the water. With daggers clenched in their terrible teeth they swam toward him. Their dark eyes remained fixed on him. He had more than once eyed a good rare steak the same way, though not, he thought, so ferally.

Cleve glanced about. He saw water, a few square feet of wooden raft. No weapons, no clothing, not even a strip of cloth or leather he might somehow turn into a means of defense. He considered diving from the raft and striking out for the opposite shore – but could Doralan Andrah swim? Which swam, the body or the brain? Because Robert Cleve could ride a bicycle, could he do so in this body? Because he was a powerful swimmer – was his host-body?

He knelt, crosswise to the raft's length, hooking his toes over the other side. He waited, watching the shaggy-headed approach of the two warriors with their teeth-gripped knives. The knives, he saw, were of flint. Whatever he was, however far he'd come, he was no longer in Doralan Andrah's purlieu. These men were savages who, like savages of his own Earth, lived still in the Stone Age.

And ate human flesh.

One swimmer soon forged ahead of the other, and Cleve sucked in a deep breath when a black-nailed hand slapped at the edge of his raft, gripping it. The man would thus support himself in the water while with the other hand he took his dagger from his teeth. The dagger the kneeling Cleve wanted. For a moment their eyes met, and then Cleve fell forward. One of his big hands was fisted, the other outstretched with open fingers. The fist smashed down on the savage's fingers. The warrior opened wide his mouth to howl, as Cleve had expected, and Cleve's other hand snatched the dagger as it dropped from filed teeth. With his toes over the other edge of the raft, balancing it however precariously, Cleve slashed out with the long flint blade. It laid open the man's forehead even as he released his grip on the raft and tried desperately to backpedal.

Cleve slid forward directly toward him, into the water, as the other swimmer upended one end of the raft. Cleve entered the water headfirst. His outstretched hands contacted the first man, he of the bloody forehead. Instantly the Andorite savage gripped him and they grappled in the water. Cleve striving to use the dagger. His gasping head surfaced and he rolled his eyes to see the other man swimming close, his dagger now in his hand. It hampered his swimming, but he was ready to sip the blood of the naked raft man. Desperately Cleve rolled, gripping his opponent, and felt the man shudder as his own compatriot drove his knife into his back in a blow intended for Cleve. Cleve kicked free, striving at once to retain his grip on his newly acquired dagger, to keep himself afloat, and to get clear of the jerking, floundering body of the dying man – and out of reach of his enraged fellow.

Behind him sounded more splashes. He knew their meaning without glancing: More enemies were swimming out either to slay him or force him ashore to their cookpots – if they cooked their meat. He drew a breath and dived.

All that happened thereafter took place far more swiftly than it can be described.

He arced beneath the surface of Sky River, making the constant physical effort always required to open his eyes underwater. Before him were legs, two churning, two lifeless, in pink-stained water. Knowing there were too many for him to attempt to fight, Cleve wheeled underwater, twisting to swim for the shore opposite that controlled by his Stone Age enemies.

Coming directly toward him, hair streaming out about their dark heads, were two of the savages. They separated slightly to come at him from two directions. Again he made an instantaneous decision, and he hurled himself forward beneath the water in an attempt to drive between them.

Undoubtedly by pure accident, the foot of a swimmer above him trod Cleve's head. He was swung slightly toward one of his underwater enemies – and the man whose foot had struck his head immediately shouted and upended himself to come streaking down. Cleve twisted as he neared his opponent, turning upside down in the strange slow motion of submarine activity. As he passed beneath the savage, Cleve's Stone Age dagger laid open the other's belly. There was a hard wrench when the blade struck the man's belt – and then the weapon was dragged from Cleve's grasp.

Hopelessly, already in need of air, he turned back to try to take one of the others down to death with him. He had found adventure on Andor, and excitement, and danger – and the death Gordon had warned him of.

His eyes went wide. The strange colors, the monster sun, the enormous, riotously colored flowers and trees and ferns, the savages with their filed teeth – all these were as everyday occurrences compared to what he now saw. He and his cannibalistic attackers were not alone in their silent arena beneath the river's surface. One of them was already twisting downward, his dagger falling free. His chest streamed a scarlet cloud that became rapidly pink in the water. Another was hurling himself up to the surface, his eyes bulging in what Cleve thought – with amazement – was fear.

A third was grappling with the newcomer.

She was a lithe, muscular girl with long white hair streaming out behind her like a fringed cloak.

The hair was white, not blond; that was obvious even in its present wet state, although its owner was just as obviously a very young woman. Stranger still were her hands and feet: Her fingers and toes, he saw with disbelief, were webbed! Her toes were almost nonexistent, little lumps protruding from the webbing at the ends of long, wedge-shaped feet. And – her right hand was finned. No, Cleve realized, seeing the bindings of what looked like gut; she but wore a six-inch fin strapped to her palm. With it she had obviously slain one of his attackers, frightened off another, and was even now slashing a third. She wore slightly less than her opponent; bare of ornamentation, her nudity was adorned only with a slender strip of black about her hips; it was of some glistening stuff he could not identify. There was no sheath, and Cleve supposed she merely thrust her fin knife into the thong, or perhaps tied it there by the same straps with which it was bound to her palm.

Batting aside a fourth attacker, Cleve propelled himself rapidly toward her. She had come to his rescue; now she needed help. His hands gripped the ankles of the man she fought; jerked. The girl slashed the savage's throat open, and for a moment her eyes met Cleve's. Hers, he saw, were completely colorless: great black pupils seemingly afloat in elongated circles totally devoid of coloration.

Then her gaze leaped past him, and those strange, fishlike eyes went wider.

He started instantly to flail himself into a roll, knowing by her gaze and her reaction that another enemy was streaking down behind him. This, he knew, would be the last of them he'd face, or try to face. His strained lungs would burst in another few seconds. Whoever she was, whatever she was, wherever she had come from, his strange aide was too late. And there were too many foes, even had she been a man, or armed with a spear gun – had there been spear guns on Andor.

Even while the hopeless thoughts seared his mind, he was wriggling around to meet his armed enemy as best he could with bare hands. Then a cold, strong hand closed about his wrist. He was yanked downward. And down and down, until the water was dark and he felt pressure, felt himself weakening. His head roared and the blood strove to burst through his throbbing temples and his heart shrieked within him for release from the impossible burden.

His lungs gave up. The water was darker, much darker, but he was certain the dark was behind his eyes. He exhaled, trying to stretch it out, knowing he would inhale at once. He was beyond caring. His eyes bulged. His head roared and pounded. They seemed to be entering an underwater tunnel of some sort, but the last of the air streamed from Cleve's lungs and bubbled upward through the darkling waters.

Chapter Eight

The Mermaid of Orisana

Robert Cleve regained consciousness with a pounding headache, a sore chest, and an intensely sore throat. He lay on his back in a dark, wet place whose air was dank and fetid. But – it was air. Heaven, he was convinced, would be more pleasant and Hell would be worse. In which case he was most probably alive.

'Am I alive?'

A feminine giggle, from a young throat. Then she spoke, in an accent so extreme he barely understood her. Universal language, Gordon had said, and it had not occurred to Cleve that that was not so marvelous and simple as it sounded. His native tongue on Earth was English, but he spoke American, not English, England and America, Bernard Shaw had observed, were two countries separated by a common language. Not only did the accents differ, even within each nation, but there were divergent word meanings as well as idioms. Then there was Australia, speaking the same language – sort of – and Canada. Cleve wondered: What was the universal language of Andor like on the other side of this planet?

'You are alive,' the accented voice from the darkness said, and a soft hand caressed his chest. 'So long as you can talk, Skyman, you are alive.'

He smiled in the blackness. 'Skyman?'

'You come from above, but you are not of the Treemen. Your teeth are different, and your hair, and they are your enemies. You are not of the water, though, as I am, nor of the trees. You must be from the sky.'

He chuckled. 'I guess I am, come to think, and a lot farther up than you think! My name is—' He hesitated. He had two names now. And Doralan Andrah was apparently a man of some importance. But – this was not his land. 'My name is Cleve,' he told her, for the first time realizing that Doralan had been of some value, anyhow; at least this body could swim!

'Cleve? Rich air, Cleve. I am Siraa.'

'I owe you this life, Siraa,' he said, wondering at what had sounded like a ritual greeting: 'Rich air.' His phrasing, too, was ritual: 'I owe you this life,' not 'my life,' among a people who knew, as most of Earth did, that there had been lives before this one and that more would follow in the ring of reincarnated return. 'Where are we, Siraa?'

'In – oh, you don't know at all. We entered an underwater cavern. Beneath the river. The passageway into the shore angles up sharply, until it is above the water level. You were unconscious when we surfaced in here, but I expelled most of the water from your lungs – you took but half a watery breath, I think.'

He nodded, though she could not see. The blackness was total, and her words explained why. They explained, too, the closeness, and dampness, the thin quality of the air – as well as her greeting, 'Rich air.' They were in something akin to an alligator den – or was it crocodile? They were under the water – but they weren't.

He was sure the question was hardly worth asking, remembering her appearance:

'Is this where you live, Siraa?'

Again the liquid giggle. 'It is a road to where I live, yes. We do not live in darkness, Skyman Cleve. We live beneath you, and enter Orisana only via the water, but we have light in our city.'

City! Orisana: 'water land.' Yes. *Be prepared for anything,* he told himself. *Accept anything. Mermaids and merpeople – why not, on Andor?*

'Are you taking me to your people, Siraa? To Orisana?'

'Oh, no! They would kill you, or at best enslave you. There are but a few *others* among us, some of the Treemen, and Oridorns. All are slaves. No – I will take you back, up through the water, to the shore opposite the Treemen – I have never seen any of them on the other side. But – as you said, you owe me this life, Cleve. I lay claim.'

Into the total darkness he said, 'To my life?'

'Oh, no!' She was suddenly close against him, all young feminine curves and soft hands, and he learned what he had not noticed in the water. He could not stifle a shudder; her flesh was cold!

'No, Skyman Cleve. I – I have watched the Treemen; long I've watched in fascination, even though they are little more than beasts. But – the pretty color of their skin, and their hair and eyes – and yours. Today I saw you, and came to help. I do not want your life – you must give me only *of* your life. Warm me, with the warmth you people from above possess in your bodies.' And she snuggled close.

Cold or not, she was passionate and intensely female in the darkness, and he warmed her, giving her a small measure of his life while she crooned and clung tightly to him.

Then she sighed and rose, clinging to his hand, warm with the warmth he had injected, and suddenly there was light, flickering and yellow, and she voiced a little cry and squeezed his hand in her chill one.

'Siraa!' The voice was male. 'We were – ah! You've brought us one of those from above! It is a muscular one – is it alive?'

Cleve rolled over, then rose slowly to face the possessor of the new voice.

Five of them crowded the underground passage that rose behind them in the darkness. There was no darkness here, not now. In his left hand each man but the first held aloft an intensely bright, radiant torch. In his right hand each held one of the white fins such as the girl had; theirs, too, were strapped into their palms. It occurred to Cleve that thus they could be constantly armed, although the carrying of the bony dagger would not interfere in the least with their swimming. Their fingers and toes, like Siraa's, were webbed, and their hair white. So was their skin very pale, as if they had never seen or felt the light of the sun; they probably had not. These people lived solely *beneath* the land, within Andor, gaining access to their Orisana only via the tunnel or tunnels into the water.

They, too, wore the thin strip of unidentifiable, glistening black about their hips, but they were not wholly nude as was

Siraa. Two more strips depended from the 'belt' attached to a pouch or codpiece covering the groin. For protection while swimming, Cleve thought, and for support. Two more straps ran down from the bottom of the codpiece each man wore, between his thighs and up in back to secure again to the belt. They wore nothing else, aside from expressions of acute unfriendliness.

The jet pupils of their round eyes looked all the blacker because of the total lack of color surrounding them. They were the strangest eyes he had ever seen. They were the eyes of fish. They all stared at Cleve.

He considered escape and discarded the idea. There was but one way to go – past the four fin-armed men into the land of Orisana. He stripped his gaze from the leader's left fist with difficulty: the Orisan held a sword, and it appeared to be steel or iron.

'It is both muscular and alive,' Cleve said quietly. 'It is also grateful. Siraa of Orisana saved me from the Treemen who sought to kill me. They are my enemies, they are your enemies. We should be friends.'

The foremost Orisan, with the metal sword, smiled. 'Friends?' He glanced at his companions. They grinned. 'It wants to be our friend,' he said, and laughed.

Siraa stepped quickly past Cleve, lifting her hands in remonstrance. 'Zivaat – this is a man, as you are. Only a little different. And you can easily see he is not of the Treefolk. He is a Skyman. The Treemen were trying to capture him. You know why. He is wondrous warm and—'

The Orisan leader, the merman she called Zivaat, twisted his face in sudden anger. His empty left hand snaked out to slap her across the face. Her long mass of white hair, still wet, flailed as she stumbled back into Cleve. He stopped her with his hands on her shoulders, steadying her. Then he set the girl aside and took a long stride forward.

Zivaat was unprepared for the attack; unprepared for the rocklike fist that slammed into his jaw. He spun half around as he staggered back into his fellows. Cleve plucked the curved sword from the dazed Orisan's hand with ease. He stepped quickly back, putting back a hand to steer Siraa out of the way. He hefted the scimitarlike weapon, getting its feel, testing its weight.

'There isn't room in this passage for all of you to come at me massed,' he snapped. 'Come one at a time, then, if you dare, and you die one at a time! Zivaat, save them. Order them not to advance!'

Half-supported by one of his men, Zivaat stared at him in obvious amazement.

'Hear me, men of Orisana. Because we live below the ground or above it, because there are some few physical differences between us . . . these are not reasons for us to be enemies. I am as much a stranger and enemy to those cannibals you call Treemen as you. I come from far to the north. We have no quarrel. Siraa befriended me, saved my life. Allow me to visit you, or leave you, as you wish. But let us do it in peace.' He looked at none of them save Zivaat.

'But – you are not one of us,' Zivaat said. 'You are not *like* us! We – how can we be friends? We are men, and you—'

Cleve smiled. 'I am a man also,' he said. 'Something happened, long ago. Your people were perhaps trapped here. Without sun, your hair and skin lost its pigmentation. I can't explain your eyes, but because you must swim to leave your underground homes, you developed webbing on your hands and feet.' He shrugged. 'We're both men, Zivaat. Just . . . slightly different. Men need not always be enemies, because they are different.'

Zivaat continued to stare. If anything his huge, pellucid eyes were wider; something Cleve had said had horrified the merman. Cleve wondered what he could possibly have said to be so offensive. Then Zivaat spun, to tear a torch from the hand of one of his followers. Almost in the same motion, almost without pausing, the merman swung back. The unnaturally bright torch whooshed as it rushed at Cleve's face. He threw up an arm and ducked, going to one knee to avoid the flying firebrand. Behind him, Siraa shrieked. He wheeled quickly, thinking the hurled torch must have struck her.

It had not. She was struggling desperately, hopelessly, against a wet black cable the thickness of Cleve's arm. It was wrapped twice about her lithe body, rising up the declivity from the water below, and something was pulling it steadily tighter. Black and wet and glistening, it vanished down into the darkness.

'Llico!' one of the men cried. 'A llico has Siraa!'

It was then Cleve realized there was no man down there, pulling Siraa down; it was a river monster, a creature with at least one long, black tentacle! Now he saw it, or at least he spotted its head; three yellow eyes seemed to iridesce in the blackness down the incline. The woman was being pulled down to them, and whatever jaws went with them.

Again she shrieked, and Cleve's movement was pure reflex. He got to his feet, swinging up the scimitar as he sprang toward her. The sword flashed down, and his arm quivered as the blade struck the thick tentacle with a wet, chunking sound. The sword bit half through the ropy black arm, bringing a roar as of a dozen lions from the darkness below. Cleve had to lay hold of the hilt with both hands to free his sword, amid a welter of indigo ichor that bubbled up from the wound. He swung up his blade and struck again.

Inexpert, he did not land his great chopping blow in the same place. He cut a new slice deep into the tentacle. Again he had to wrench his blade free. Siraa's screams had stilled; even wounded, the powerful tentacle gripped her so tightly she could no longer muster the breath to cry out. Robert Cleve swung back the sword – and nearly fell. Another ropy tentacle had snaked up from the blackness, broken only by those three xanthous eyes, to snap around his ankle. Once, twice, three times the terrible cable wrapped, and it was cold, cold as death. And strong, tightening. He felt his leg start to throb.

He ignored the new menace, the danger to himself, slashing down again at the octopoid arm enwrapping Siraa's slender waist. This time he clove through it. Purple ichor gouted as the severed black arm plopped to the hard-packed, damp floor of the tunnel.

Suddenly released, Siraa lurched and spun up the acclivity toward her rescuer. She fell, tearing away with her hands that portion of the tentacle still enwrapping her.

Dragged down by the tentacular cable about his ankle,

Cleve tried to shift, to chop down at it. He slipped, fell. Immediately he felt himself dragged powerfully down toward those unblinking yellow eyes and the terrible mouth he knew must accompany them.

He heard the cries, saw the flash of hairless white legs past his face. He heard the thwocking sound of sword biting into pulpy flesh. The tentacle loosened about his ankle, then tightened spasmodically. Realizing that someone had yanked the scimitar from his fingers and was using it to save his life, Cleve fought to stay conscious against the pain searing up his leg. Again the sound of sword sinking into the river monster's serpentine arm. This time Cleve knew the second tentacle had been chopped from the creature the mermen called a 'llico.'

Strong hands seized his wrists and he was jerked up the damp incline while again the monster roared from the darkness below.

No one seemed to notice as the Orisan who had jerked the sword from Cleve's hand to save him with it – now returned it to him!

Cleve lay on the damp, slippery floor of the inclined cavern and watched as two thrown torches whooshed downward. For an instant he saw the globate, black head with its three yellow eyes, the gaping, many-fanged mouth. Then one of the torches vanished into that hideous maw, and the creature's roar became a shriek. It shot backward and disappeared. The second torch lay on the glistening wet ground, flickering.

Slowly Robert Cleve looked up. Then down at his sword. He dropped it. He held up his empty hand.

'I am Cleve. I owe you this life.'

'I am Vilaat. I free you from debt. You saved Siraa.' The man who had chopped him free accepted his hand and helped him up. He stepped between Cleve and the leader, Zivaat.

'Cleve is my friend,' Vilaat said.

Zivaat looked past the man, over his shoulder at Cleve. He nodded. 'Cleve is our friend.'

‘I offer apology for striking Zivaat,’ Cleve said, ‘and bow my head to challenge and invective.’

‘Foregone,’ Zivaat said. For a moment they gazed at each other; Vilaat stepped aside. Moving slowly, Cleve bent and picked up the sword he had snatched from Zivaat’s hand. He returned it.

‘Shall I come with you to Orisana? I’d like to prevail on you for some food,’ Cleve said, suddenly feeling extremely hungry.

Zivaat frowned a little: the Orisans exchanged looks.

‘Yes,’ Zivaat said. ‘Come.’

Wondering at the glances, Cleve followed the mermen and the one remaining torch up the incline. At his side walked the strange-eyed, web-digited girl Siraa, her hip rubbing his at every other step. Ahead lay darkness, and somewhere within the earth – the andor – lay Orisana, subterranean city of the merpeople.

Chapter Nine

The Underground City of Orisana

They were short on imagination, the merpeople of the subterranean land of Orisana. But Cleve could not condemn them. They were Stone Age folk who had never seen the sun. They subsisted on fish and mushrooms and the strange orange fruits that grew in their underground demesne. Stone Age, but they were not barbaric, although their 'clothing' was little more than ornamentation. What other need was there, in a land of alwayswarmth? Only a need dictated by an antipeople religion, which they did not seem to possess – or be possessed by. Architecture? There was none.

Cleve wondered how it had got here, this Brobdingnagian cavern. It stretched for miles; if it had always been here, surely it had been widened by men, or perhaps dividing walls knocked laboriously out to connect the many tunnels that had existed here, time out of mind.

Centuries? How long, Cleve mused, had the Orisans been here? What had they been like, in the beginning? Natural evolution was not the only explanation for their differences, he was certain. True, they had no need of pigmentation in hair or skin or iris here, where the sun never shone. But they really had little need of webbed digits, just as the women of the western portion of Earth had no need of the breasts they no longer used to nourish their offspring. Perhaps the Orisans were far older than Orisana. Perhaps they had been aquatics, long, long ago.

A possible cause of mutation was obvious here, and Cleve stared about and up at it.

Orisana existed in twilight, permanent twilight, rather than subterranean darkness. The walls of the enormous cavern glowed. What luminous substance was there Cleve had no way of knowing; perhaps it emitted radiation, perhaps it did not. But . . . if it did . . . then the physical strangeness of the

Orisans was explained. They were radioactive mutants! And – he was in danger here.

Not until much later was he to learn more about the source of the luminescence, and its extraordinary properties.

Orisana was a twilight city existing upon rock, beneath rock, within rock, walled by rock. It was a vast openness, with no structures marring the grassless underground plain. It was dotted with boulders and rocks in many shapes, that plain. The few structures were poor things of peeled wood brought here laboriously from above, down through the water. And there was much use of fishbone, and scaly 'hides,' and gut, or strips of fishhide. There was much use, too, of the leathery black outer flesh of the river monster they called Ilico, and of other parts of its huge body, including bone, and whole, dried tentacles. The rocks and boulders had been cut, sanded, planed, pierced – God, he mused, how long that must take them, with nothing to work with but bone and fin and rock!

The 'city' was within the walls. The dwellings were in the scores, hundreds of dark tunnels radiating from the huge central cavern. Many of them were well above floor level (or plain level). These were reached by steps cut into the rock, or by ladders made of poles and bones, bound with gut and Ilico tentacles, or strips from the Ilico's leathery hide.

Cleve knew they had ascended, he and the mermaid Siraa and the mermen Zivaat and Vilaat and the other three pale-eyed, white-haired, white-skinned Orisans. But, he thought, looking up, surely they had not been down so far as to account for that vastly high ceiling!

No, they must be within a mountain, with natural tunnels – old watercourses – leading out into the river.

They came clustering about him, and the Orisans with him were kept busy explaining over and over that he was guest, not captive. He ignored the taunts and insults of those who trouped to them, ignored them as best he could. People were always braver in concert, more bold and ready to insult and spit and strike and hurl whatever came to hand – if that sort of cowardice could be called bravery. They were always more willing, too, to hurl their invective and missiles at those who were *different* – and even more particularly when he who was different was naked, unarmed, and surrounded by armed guards.

His tormentors, of course, were few; most in Orisana were too busy to waste time trying to elevate themselves by pretending that another was lower.

Zivaat and Vilaat had accepted him without reservation. True, their accent was strange, but they spoke Andoran, the almost-universal language of this planet. And at least some of their customs were the same as those outside their self-contained world.

'I owe you this life,' Cleve had said ritually, for this was knowledge implanted in his brain on Earth, not necessarily a part of the memory of Doralan Andrah, the memory he did not possess.

'I free you from debt,' Vilaat had replied. It had been the Orisan's decision to make; he could have said, 'I lay claim,' meaning that Cleve must grant him a boon, even the life itself. Since Vilaat had saved that life, it was his, until he either returned it to Cleve by pronouncing the words 'I free you from debt' or until the debt was discharged to his satisfaction. He might well have said, as may have been expected, 'I defer claim.' This would have meant that he did indeed make claim but would press it later, at his leisure. The saved, in honor, must accept that he would be presented with a petition by his savior – one he must grant, even if it meant his death.

It was an uncomplicated code, and a fair one. 'I free you from debt' meant just that. The savior made absolutely no claim on him he'd saved, and never would, in honor. Indeed, it would be disgraceful for him ever again to mention his having performed the service. One did not remind one's beneficiaries of one's benefactions, on Andor. On barbaric Andor, the performer of a service or favor could not remind the recipient over and over of his obligation, as was the case on civilized Earth.

Then there was the second exchange that had taken place between Robert Cleve and the fish-eyed men of Orisana.

Cleve had apologized to Zivaat for having struck him, and

had made the ritual offer, 'I bow to challenge and invective.' The words ceded the Orison the right to challenge Cleve to combat, or to call down malignancy on his head, via cursing; the expression now loosely used on his native Earth, 'Go to Hell,' had represented, in long-ago time, a serious attempt on the part of the curser to make the other genuinely accursed: to condemn him to the infernal regions. For words had power, those ancient *Habiru* of Earth had believed. Like Vilaat, Zivaat had had three choices. To challenge or curse, to defer either or both to a later time, thus keeping Cleve in his debt, on needles and pins. Or to dismiss the right, which Zivaat had done. He had foregone both rights, permanently.

Thus, Cleve's escorts were not captors, and they defended him from their people who struck and spat at him, calling out insults.

There was, he mused with a grim smile, another possible explanation. Sometimes one made no claim against a life, or forewent challenge or invective, as a gesture of contempt. The second party would not stoop so low as to challenge, to curse, or to lay claim to the paltry life of one for whom he felt – or pretended to feel – contempt.

Possibly, Robert Cleve thought. But he felt that was not the case. His words and his bravery and his prowess had won respect and friendship, or at least a truce, among the Orisan warriors.

They took him to a wide-mouthed tunnelway flanked by two men. They were armed with metal swords resembling Zivaat's weapon – which Cleve had returned. The guards were further distinguished by decoration: Blue pigment, with a look of permanency about it, had been applied to their bodies, forming five concentric circles radiating outward from their navels. One of them had also a diagonal blue line on his forehead, between his brows, which Cleve assumed set him apart as senior guard. Both men also wore the tight loin pouches worn by Cleve's escorts.

Cleve was approaching what served Orisana as palace, or governor's mansion: the two men with the swords and paint must be elite guards.

'We crave audience,' Zivaat said. 'We've a Skyman with us, named Cleve. He—'

'Skyman, Zivaat? Cleve?' The guard who spoke looked past Zivaat at the muscular, bronze man who was not of Orisana. At his side, quite close, stood Siraa.

'Why is he not bound?' he of the blue brow-stripe demanded. 'Why is he allowed such proximitity to one of Orisana's most beauteous maidens?' The Orisan guard smiled at Siraa, nodding to her. 'Shilaat has no need to see the dark-skinned creature; he's seen many. Take it over to the slave compound, get it registered, and put it to work.'

Zivaat stepped back one pace. 'Bavuraat, your memory seems to have left you. You've forgotten who you are, who I am. Don't presume to talk that way to me again, ever. Today I feel magnanimous. Next time I'll report to Shilaat that you've allowed your post to go to your head and should perhaps be assigned to overseeing quarry slaves, or . . . to Oridorn duty?'

Bavuraat stiffened. With fearful eyes, he bowed.

'Zivaat is right,' he said. 'I have allowed my elevation to this post outside Shilaat's door to affect my manners. I am indebted to Zivaat for his warning, instead of reporting me.'

'Tell Shilaat that I would speak with him, as soon as possible. Don't tell him about the Skyman – let me explain. But unless Shilaat so decrees, Cleve is not a slave.' Zivaat folded his arms in an attitude of impatient waiting.

Bavuraat looked astonished; his eyes flickered past Zivaat to Cleve. Cleve stared back. He found it hard to work up any feeling of friendship for a man who wanted to put 'it' to work as a slave. A thought crossed Cleve's mind, and he almost thought, as befit an Andorite warrior whose body he possessed: He'd love to show Bavuraat just which of them was more worthy of guarding Shilaat, whoever he was, and which belonged in servitude!

The guard entered the broad doorway into the rock.

They waited in silence. Cleve watching the passing of an Orisan chain gang. Five of the slaves were obviously the cannibals called Treemen, although he did not see their faces; pigmented men stood out very brightly among a monochromatic people. The other three were even whiter than the Orisans, with hair so pale it was almost transparent; long and unkempt. Beside them marched three Orisans with fins strapped to their palms. One carried a desiccated Ilico tentacle; it must serve him as a whip. Cleve did not see the faces of the snowy slaves.

'Shilaat will see you now,' Bavuraat said, and Cleve swung his head to see that the guard had returned from within the rock.

Zivaat entered first, followed by Vilaat, the merman who'd saved Cleve's life. Then Cleve, closely followed by Siraa – who looked shocked and refused violently when he waved to her to precede him. Women are low among them, he thought; it is usually thus, once people progress to the point of learning to connect the magic of a woman's childbearing with the man. Priorly, she was elevated, revered, served. Once the man learned he was necessary to the process of generation, he quickly reversed the situation, punishing her, consciously or not, for having venerated her. Among the Orisans, as among most of the people of Andor, women were chattels.

Except of course, the Starpowered witches.

The others remained outside; once he was within the side cavern, Cleve heard the guard Bavuraat demand to know what was so special about that muscle-bound Treeman with the weird hairdo. Cleve put up his hand to feel. For the first time he discovered that his hair was drawn back into a sort of thick pigtail, bound by a metal band. Behind him Siraa chuckled and touched him; she must have thought he was preening before meeting the Great Man. He wished he'd kept his big hand down.

They were in a tunnel, and it wound. The luminous substance in the walls of the main cavern was not present here, and torches were set into the walls at brief intervals, on alternate sides. Gauging the intervals at three yards, he counted seventeen torches and eight turns before they reached the wider portion of the cavern: Shilaat's chamber. In it was a broad, smooth slab of green-veined marble three feet high, behind which a smaller slab was piled with Ilico hides and topped with some silken pelt of snowy white. On this sat Shilaat.

He appeared to be a tall Orisan, with thinning hair, few lines in his paper-white face, and the growing belly that marked most executives, anywhere. His questioning smile faded as he caught sight of the man behind Zivaat.

'I was not told you were bringing an Overworld slave with you, Zivaat. No slave has ever entered here before. And who comes behind – ah! Who is this?' Shilaat's expression of displeasure vanished as he gazed at Siraa.

'Siraa, Shilaat, hoping it pleases. She aided the Skyman Cleve when he was attacked by the Treemen,' Zivaat explained. 'He saved her from one of them, and later, under our eyes, he saved her from a llico, using my sword – which he then returned, although we had promised him only slavery. He is not a Treeman, Shilaat, and he has saved Siraa, one of Orisana's loveliest maidens. And – he thinks. Tell him what you told me about strangers, Cleve – *not* about *why* there are differences, but that there are, and about slavery and trust and friendship.'

'I understand,' Cleve said, wondering why he was told so specifically to eschew his explanation of the Orisan's origin. 'May I have the permission of the thrice-noble Shilaat to speak?'

'Thrice-noble,' Shilaat repeated. And he smiled. 'Yes, speak, you with the tongue of light.' Not 'golden-tongued'; light was more precious to these dwellers within the ground than the soft yellow metal so prized elsewhere by those so rich they were less impressed with real values.

Cleve repeated his words about color and difference; the words he'd spoken to Zivaat just before he'd somehow stirred the merman's ire. Then the story was told, and even Siraa, despite her station as a woman, was allowed to tell what she knew of the strange, colorful man from the Overworld. To his complete astonishment and embarrassment, she told everything. Shilaat even touched him to feel his warmth, although he was certainly as aware as Cleve and Siraa that he could never fully appreciate that warmth as had the Orisan woman.

'Cleve, where are you from? What do you call yourself?'

'Do you know the name Doralan Andrah?'

Shilaat's blank look was mirrored in the faces of the others. Cleve sighed and shrugged.

'My name is Robert Cleve. I am from Earth. I am called an American.'

'Erth? Uhmaireekun?' Shilaat of Orisana shrugged. 'I suppose it isn't unusual that I have never heard those names. We are aware of the broad world above, but remain here in safety. Your teeth indicate that not all men of the Overworld eat people?'

'Oh, no,' Cleve said, smiling to give Shilaat a good, reassuring look at his unsharpened teeth. 'The Treemen eat people, as you know, and the government of Russia is based on the eating of people, and of China. But these represent a small portion of the total population, Shilaat.' Cleve thought of the people-eaters among his own people, on his own planet, and he winced. There were many. Some of them did worse than merely eat their fellowmen; they chewed them up and spat them out and then sat on the pieces, hardly deigning to notice that they were there. The cannibal, at least, ate for a purpose.

'Are all the people of the Overworld as you are, Cleve? With colors, I mean?'

Cleve shook his head. 'The greatest percentage are brown, or black, or yellow,' he said. 'There are but a few so pale as I.' He spoke as a 'white' man, nearly forgetting that on Orisan he was reddish-bronze.

Looking concerned, Shilaat nevertheless nodded. 'They rule?'

'They're working on it,' Cleve told him.

'And . . . white people,' Shilaat asked. 'Are there many of us?'

'Shilaat, there are many people of my world who *think* they are white.' He looked down at his bronze body. No, he'd seen people return from Florida vacation with deeper color than this. And return to rule discriminatorily over people actually lighter than themselves – people they called black.

He broke the news to the first white man he had ever seen, aside from albinos:

'No. Shilaat. None is so fair as your people. But I assure you that those who call themselves white would find a reason for hating you. Because you ARE white, perhaps. More likely because of your hair and toes and eyes.'

Shilaat nodded. 'You are telling me that my people are better off precisely where they are, separated from the Over-world of evil. We know that. Is "American" its capital?'

Cleve grinned. 'No, but . . . go ahead and think of it in that way, I don't mind. And yes, I suppose you're better off here in' – he glanced around – 'Camelot. Or Birchland, maybe. You ask these things, Shilaat – have you never before had someone here from, uh, outside?'

'Only the Treemen,' Shilaat said. 'And they are . . . savages, eaters of human flesh, barbaric in their habits. And filthy. You are not of them; you are far different. They are more like animals. You are more like . . . us.'

'I remind you,' Cleve said, smiling, 'that both you and Zivaat had referred to me as "it" and thought only of enslaving me – because I am different from you.'

Shilaat regarded the top of his marble desk. Then he looked up. 'Cleve of Earth is my friend and guest,' he said, and to Cleve: 'We will dine together. He is to be treated as nothing less than an honored noble of Orisan. He will . . . advise me.' He looked at Cleve. Cleve smiled, inclining his head. Shilaat smiled. His eyes shifted to the slender but muscular girl at Cleve's side.

'Do you have family, Siraa?'

She nodded.

'Then I want to know your father's name. Meanwhile, Cleve American will live with your family. Cleve American of Earth – is this satisfactory?'

Cleve nodded, delighted. 'Pai,' he agreed. 'But in light of the things we've said to each other, calling me "American" seems small. I am Cleve of Earth. That's enough. And – I am honored and pleased to be so well treated and assigned by the thrice-noble Shilaat of Orisana.'

The thrice-noble Shilaat of Orisana bowed his bald head

with a little smile. Then he raised his hands to remove the necklace he wore, apparently as a mark of rank. Lifting it over his head, he indicated to Cleve that he was to bow his. Cleve did.

'This will prevent any of my people from mistaking you for a slave, Cleve of Earth.' The gaze of his colorless eyes went past Cleve. 'Zivaat, I am assigning you as Cleve's guide. Siraa . . . come to dinner with our guest.'

Which was how Robert Cleve of Earth, imprisoned within the body of Doralan Andrah of Andor, came by his rattling necklace of snowy fish teeth stung on a strip of the black, leathery hide of the llico.

Chapter Ten

The People in the Mountain

Though the Orisans were not troubled with artificial modesty, they did cover – or decorate – themselves when out of the water they loved. In addition to the pouchlike groin coverings they wore, the men adorned themselves with bone jewelry and bits of agate, as well as sashes composed of some sort of hide covered with long, soft white hair or fur, extremely fine and silky. Siraa donned a breechclout of the same fur, slung very low on her slender hips. Around her neck glittered a necklace whose quartzlike azure stones must have required years of digging and laborious chipping. Cleve could not avoid watching them twinkle between her breasts as they crossed to Shilaat's private cavern for dinner. They were stared at, they and their two-man escort, and Cleve felt sure the gazes were as much attracted by Siraa's lithe loveliness as by his strangeness. Together, they were the cynosure of all Orisana.

With his deep-bronzed skin, his glossy black hair so dark it gleamed with blue highlights, and his eyes like granite, he felt gaudy among these achromatic people.

They were disturbingly uniform: skin the color of paper and appearing as thin, hair like mountain snow, eyes like black buttons floating in a poll of pellucid water. All the men wore the loin pouches; most of the females who'd reached the nubile stage wore the low-slung trunks of white fur, resembling pelts from the haughty, overpampered Persian cats of his native planet. Whence came they, he wondered. Fur, in this marvelous warm haven within the very planet? Obviously, they were unnecessary; if there were animals making their sunless homes within these caverns, they had no need of fur! Nor would any denizens of the jungle bordering the river outside require such silken pelts. And . . . white? No, no jungle creature would have been provided by their creator with such coloration, guaranteed to be unprotective amid the gorgeous verdure outside.

Unless – and Cleve was beginning to suspect – unless the god of Andor was insane.

Dinner in the regal cavern of Shilaat, Grof of Orisana, consisted of mushrooms, small, rather dry fruits, and four kinds of fish. It was served by two slaves clad from neck to toe in extraordinarily loose gowns of deep, rich purple. The skin of the servants was even more pale, Cleve saw, than that of his hosts. There was a tissuelike quality about their almost transparent flesh, so thin and pale it was bluish, showing clearly its network of veins. Their hair fell in clouds like the angel's hair of an Earthy Christmas tree, in rippling waves. Here was one people, Cleve was sure, who could truthfully say there was nothing to be done with their hair!

But their hair, their skin, their long, long fingers with the transparent nails – these were far from the most unusual features of Shilaat's almost matched pair of slaves.

The two women were eyeless.

Not just blind, not just sightless; eyeless.

The bone structure, the barely defined sockets; these indicated that they had once possessed eyes, but not for many generations.

Cleve restrained himself from querying Shilaat about the women – Gaise and Jaire – until they had finished their serving and retired at a word from their master.

'Oridorns,' Shilaat replied. 'Oridorna lies above us, also within the mountain. But they cannot leave, as we can. Even had they eyes, they would never see the great skyfire that burns us so, and their caverns have no lights in the living rock, as have ours.'

Cleve frowned. He was within a mountain, then. And Orisana, 'water land,' was merely the lower keep. Above it, in another cavern system, lay another people. Oridorna: 'rock land.' Cut off by the Orisans themselves from egress through the watery channel the Orisans used. And somehow prevented, too, from leaving via another route. Trapped forever, within this mountain; to be born, to live, to die in total eternal darkness, without ever drawing one breath of fresh air rich with the scents of the jungle along Sky River – so close.

Thus cut off, compelled to live out their stagnant existences in complete lightlessness, the xanthochroid people of Oridorna had lost the need for eyes. And then, like the weird fish deep in Kentucky's Mammoth Cave on Earth, they had lost the eyes themselves.

Yet the women had seemed to move with sure grace, never once touching wall or table, setting down the glazed stone plates or bowls with nothing that remotely resembled a clatter or hard thump. And they kept their mouth open, both of them.

'The Oridorns would like to be here, in the light, nearer the water,' Shilaat said. 'We hold them back. Fortunately for us, neither their weapons nor their eyeless sight helps them, for they cannot invade us in any sort of mass, and we keep a constant guard posted at their three means of entry into Orisana. Occasionally we capture one, or a few. Occasionally our people are captured by them. They are of little use, save in serving and carrying.'

Eyeless sight? Cleve wondered; perhaps the Oridorns had been compensated for the theft of their eyes by some sort of innate, biological radar, such as was possessed by the bats of his own planet. He wondered. Perhaps Daron, god of Andor with His many consorts, was not insane after all. Merely . . . quixotic, whimsical, capricious.

Even though landbound in their subterranean keep, the Orisans were by necessity swimmers, and thus they had been given slender, streamlined bodies and webbing between fingers and toes to facilitate their swift passage through the water. Cursed with an enforced subterranean existence even more stringent, the Oridorns had evolved away from the eyes they did not need – but had developed some compensatory means of steering themselves around obstacles, for gauging distances.

'Why have they not sought their way out above, since you cut them off from the river tunnels?' Cleve asked.

Shilaat shook his head. 'They are surrounded, barred by solid granite of unknown thickness. In centuries of digging, our people have never broken through to the Outside. Although we have not tried to find a way out – and thus a way in for the Overworlders – we have tunneled extensively.' Carefully he drew the tiny gray bones from the yellowish meat of the little golden fish called kchan, the delicacy of which Cleve had already proven to himself. 'There is a way out – onto the mountaintop. Our Oridorn slaves tell us it is eternally cold – like the deepest water but worse.' He shrugged. 'We cannot conceive of this thing called "cold." At any rate, if they are to be believed, the mountaintop is covered always by some form of cold powdery water, white as hair.'

Cleve smiled, both at the perfectly natural simile for Orisana and at the hopelessly drab attempt to describe snow. 'You must realize they do not want to leave, Cleve. Why should they?' Shilaat spread his hands eloquently. 'Why should we? Who wants to exist beneath the fierce red skyfire, or endure the water that falls from the sky with noise like a hundred rockslides, or the fast moving air—'

'Wind?'

Shilaat nodded. 'Wind. What a terrible way to live! To be forced to *construct* caves – from trees or stones for *protection*, just to live, rather than for reasons of personal privacy.' Again the Grof of Orisana shook his head. 'How sad your people must be.'

Cleve glanced at Siraa and at his unsmiling host.

'We – have adapted,' he said. 'Humans find ways.'

'Um. Well – even if the Oridorns did wish to leave, they could not.' He lifted a bowl, set it in front of Cleve. Into it he placed a flat slab of white meat from the llico. 'Here we are,' he said. He placed another piece of llico atop the first. 'Here are the Oridorns. And—' he set a plate atop the bowl '—here are the people of Orimora, the highland. They live in the deep-piled, white, frozen water atop our mountain. They are ever at war with the Oridorns, for the Orimors would like to have the warming shelter within the mountain.'

'How do blind people fight off would-be conquerors from above them?'

Shilaat smiled and shook his head. 'They have told us,' he said, 'but we do not understand. One man among them has controlled the secret for centuries. Somehow he learned how to control the light in our walls, and made of it a weapon. Through the centuries it has been passed down from father to son. We do not understand it. But we know it exists, although we have never captured one of the devices.'

Shilaat, Cleve noticed, continually shifted his gaze to the lovely Orisan maiden – no, not maiden, not since Cleve's arrival, if she were before – the lovely Orisan beside him. Siraa ate in silence, her head usually bowed, listening to her betters. Her leg pressed the warmth of Cleve's.

He paused, in his hand a portion of the superb mushrooms that grew so abundantly here in the darker tunnels and chambers. It occurred to him that he would never leave Orisana by travelling upward or outward, seeking the sun. The only way out was up the long incline on the west, then through one of those black tunnels, then down into the pool at its other end and thence out onto Sky River's bed. From there he must kick himself upward to Sky River's surface – and then into the jungle with its cannibalistic savages and – what else?

'When I leave, then—'

'Leave?' Shilaat cocked his head. 'Why ever would you wish to leave Orisana, Cleve of Earth?'

Cleve smiled, aware of Siraa's gaze. 'Because I am not Cleve of Orisana,' he said. 'I love the sun, and the rain, and the wind. My skin is naturally pigmented to withstand the sun. My people are out there.' He shrugged. 'I will enjoy my visit, Shilaat, but – I must of course leave.'

'I understand your desire to be with your own people,' Shilaat said. 'Though I admit I cannot understand your desire to leave tranquil Orisana for the terrible world outside.'

'Shilaat, the metal sword Zivaat has. Where does it come from?'

'We have captured several of them from the Oridorns – who had them from the Orimors.'

Cleve nodded, thinking excitedly. Certainly men living in the deep snow atop a mountain had not learned to smelt iron! That they could have learned to create the obviously high-carbon metal of Zivaat's scimitar – that was more than incredible. The Orimors, then, had the weapons from elsewhere – but of far more interest: else *who*! Some sort of commerce, or perhaps merely the contact of battle, took place between the mountaintop men and an advanced people. Cleve felt his heart quicken in excitement. It brought new, prickly warmth to his body.

Perhaps there was contact between the Orimors and the people of Doralan Andrah!

Involuntarily, he glanced upward. Up there. Oridorna, land of the blind, and then Orimora, and then . . . what? Down the mountain. That was all he had to do!

All!

Hopelessly, he wondered how long it would take him to reach the steel maker via the tunnel, the river, and the jungle.

'Are you promised, Siraa?'

Shilaat's question seemed to take the young woman as much by surprise as it did Cleve. Their heads snapped up together.

'No, Shilaat.'

'Do you have a mate in the Overworld, Cleve of Earth?'

Cleve shook his head. He assumed Andrah had no wife. But then he had a second thought; he should have said yes! But – for all he knew, custom among the Orisans called for lynching, or the local equivalent, of a married man who warmed a local damsel.

Shilaat posed the question he had anticipated with dread: 'Do you desire Siraa?'

'I – of course,' Cleve said – there was no other reply he could make with her sitting there. 'All men desire Siraa, surely.' Cleve decided to push it: 'As Shilaat must.'

Shilaat bowed his head over his food, and Cleve realized he had embarrassed his host. Yes, Shilaat desired the woman, more than somewhat.

'The grof is taken with you,' he told Siraa later, after the meal and the conversation had ended – or rather run down.

'Taken—'

'Smitten. He – desires you.'

She lifted a pale shoulder. 'Many desire me. But Shilaat cannot seek another mate for five more periods; his mourning time is but half over. Oh – you don't know, of course. His mate was killed five periods ago – rockfall in their living cavern. Cleve I do not understand. You accepted me. You told the grof that you desire me – but you said also that you want to leave.'

He walked on in silence. He wondered, in the always-lit great cavern of Orisana, if it were day or night. To him it was night; he was walking a girl home from a date – neither of them wearing enough to comprise underwear for many women of his world!

'Of course, Siraa. I am of the Overworld – a Skyman, as you say. My skin, my hair, my eyes, my feet and hands, these mark me here. But beyond that – our blood is different. Mine keeps me warm. You have no need of inner warmth, the light from the rock provides it for you. Yes, I must go. And that I must go does not mean that I like you less. You understand?'

'I – I don't think so,' she said in a low, sad voice, and in silence they approached the triple-forked cavern of her parents, ten rungs above the floor of the main cavern.

He hesitated to allow her to precede him up the ladder, then, starting to follow, wished he had not. Her sinuousness was almost serpentine. He concentrated on watching the rung before his eyes, reaching up blindly for the next. When he reached the top, he found her waiting for him, and he saw that those colorless Orisan eyes were equipped with lachrymal glands. Tears sparkled on her cheeks like perfect, round diamonds.

'Cleve . . . until you go . . you will warm me?'

'Siraa, I—'

She was suddenly hard against him, clutching her face against his chest. 'You – are – sooo – warm!'

Cleve sighed, and with her cold hand in his, entered the darkness of the tunnel leading to her cave room.

Chapter Eleven

The Man of Two Worlds

Getting off to himself, alone with his thoughts, was not easy for the only bronze-skinned man in Orisana. He was treated sometimes as the alien he was, sometimes as a hated enemy, sometimes as a bright bauble to be admired and gazed at – and fondled. Many of these people had never been out of their subterranean keep. Many had never seen the river, much less the sun – which they feared. His eyes, his skin, his hair, his fingers and toes entranced them; his warmth enthralled them. They were like children, bright-eyed and babbling, extending long, pale fingers to touch him. He began to have an inkling of how it felt to be one of Earth's singing idols. Or, he mused, noticing the expressions on the white faces of the females of Orisana, a sex idol.

One custom in Orisana existed in some areas of Robert Cleve's own planet. Precisely how these people knew when it was siesta time, he did not know. There was no sun, and there was always light in Orisana. But time existed, and it was measured. At a precise time after noon – noon? – they ate, and everything seemed to stop. The lines of rock-carrying slaves were herded into the well-guarded detention tunnel and did not return. The people seemed to vanish, even the children. The constant babble, the strange hollow sound of many talking voices confined within the rock-enclosed world that was Orisana, was suddenly no longer present.

The girl Siraa had gone, with another girl and four boys, on a fruit-gathering mission. Outside, Cleve had been invited; Cleve had demurred. He was here, in a strange, granite-locked land of strange people, human but . . . not quite human. He wanted to walk in their midst, listen to them, watch them work, see their crafts. And to think.

Not until the daily siesta-time was he able to get off to

himself. Even then he had to trick his guide – guard? – Zivaat.

Cleve had noted the dark, ascending tunnel into which no one went. When the plain of Orisana was quite empty, he turned to Zivaat.

'Why didn't you tell me?'

Zivaat smiled. 'You did not ask. My orders are explicit – those Shilaat gave me in private, you understand. I am to guide. I am to observe you, of course, I am sure you realize that. But I am not to interfere with your activities – if possible. We do not want to force our daily rest on you.' He shrugged. 'Nor am I tired.'

Cleve grinned. 'Well, I admit to needing a sort of rest, Ziv. I – I've got to relieve myself.'

'Oh – I'm sorry.' Zivaat's face showed his embarrassment, cold-blooded creature or not.

Entering the tunnel mouth Zivaat indicated, Cleve took the first side passage, then the next. They were marked, these Orisan tunnelways, and he turned into the first one with the two white marks on the rock. He emerged onto the sprawling underground 'plain' twenty paces behind Zivaat. Cleve had moved perhaps thirty paces backards when Zivaat went to the mouth of the relief tunnel. He peered in, then entered. The Orisan had decided his charge had taken too long, Cleve decided, and gone in after him.

'Sorry, Zivaat,' he muttered. 'I won't get into any mischief – but I've probably got you a chewing out, just the same.'

Then he turned and sprinted.

He entered the unused cave, following its gentle ascent. He rounded a bend, skirted a rock rearing taller than he and six times as thick, and took another turn. He came upon one of the little underground streams that provided the Orisans with water.

Then, in darkness, he sat on the rock floor. Doralan Andrah's body did not want a cigarette, but Robert Cleve did. He chuckled. He could forget *that*! – and a lot of other things.

I am Robert Cleve, he told himself. *Once I was from a place called Louisville. Then I was from Kentucky. And America. Now – now I'm from Earth. But I'm not on Earth. Louisville is separated from me by a ridiculous inconceivable called parsecs. Who can possibly conceive of 19,200,000,000,000 miles, much less multiply it? What difference does it make how many miles, how many zeroes there are?*

None. It made none. He was on Andor; trapped here, in another man's body. No, not another man's body; Doralan Andrah, who had been dying, was probably dead now. This body, this handsome, muscular body, was his. Robert Cleve's.

What I've got to do is start thinking of myself as Doralan Andrah. Or at least as belonging here. Alien, yes, but understandable. These people are quite human. And this is the way I have always thought man should live. Armed. Polite, on pain of duel and death. No one sneers at another unless he is sure of his individual prowess; justice is swift and final. No one can hide within a closed steel vehicle and insult others because he feels inaccessible and protected by laws. This is how Man, on Earth, achieved his greatness. The greatness he is now destroying through overcivilization, overlegislation, overconsideration. By his skill, his wits, his speed and prowess.

This is how women are meant to live, or all those psychologists I've read were insane. Not as slaves, subservient. But as helpmeets, helpmates, to man. Not as competitors – how many silly women I have seen making themselves even sillier! If they work and compete in a man's world, they strive to emulate men – a travesty. And still continue, as Stendhal said, to think with their vaginas rather than their minds. What woman can fully respect the man she controls, or be wholly happy? And no man can wholly love the woman who directs his life, surely.

An atavist, they called him on Earth. A throwback, a semibarbarian. A 'savage', a man who preferred a free life and personal justice, given and taken. And they were right. Thus – he belonged here.

I'll make it, Robert Cleve thought. *I belong here, and I'll make it here, or die here. I'll miss a lot of things – but here I will know the daily zest of living. So I haven't the memory of a man named Doralan Andrah. The challenge is even greater! I know the language, many of the customs. I know how to use a sword. I have a strong body, fast reflexes, and little timidity. What I must eventually do is find my way to wherever 'I' am from – somehow, however long it takes.*

If only he could remember the name of the place!

He glanced around the dark, narrow cavern. He would not find the Doralan homestead, sitting here in a subterranean land more removed from the world than the farthest-out dreams of the isolationists back home on Earth. Firming his lip, he corrected himself mentally. Earth was his *former* home.

He turned his head, peering up the acclivity into the darkness.

That way: the Oridorns and the Orimors, and snow; the top of an unknown mountain in the bowels of which he sat.

The other way: into the water and a jungle apparently as dense and unexplored as the Africa of the 1800s. A jungle replete, teeming with birds and insects and animals and, he assumed, serpents. And the Treemen, the cannibalistic savages belonging to the same race as Doralan Andrah, though far different. Interesting, he thought, that only savage, uncivilized peoples eat of human flesh! At last, he mused with a little frown that became a wry smile, he *thought* the Treemen were different from 'his' people!

Strive to leave here, hope to reach the surface of Sky River, with its inimical llicos – or 'allico,' to add the Andoran plural prefix? Or strive to climb out of here, past the eyeless people and the savages living in the snow and doubtless howling winds atop the mountain? Then down it to – what?

Doralan Andrah, Robert Cleve, stood. Tight-jawed, he walked back down into the strange light of Orisana's growing walls.

Behind him, the little stream chuckled nonchalantly on.

Chapter Twelve

The Plotters in the Mountain

'Has no one ever tried prying loose some of the rocklight and carrying it into those dark caverns?' Robert Cleve asked, and Shilaat nodded sadly.

'Yes, Cleve. They lost their hands.'

'What?'

'The rocklight eats flesh, like the Treemen. Within a few days, those who touch the rocklight more than casually lose their hands, as if they were eaten way by invisible flames.'

Cleve gazed at him, remembering his half-baked theory of radioactive mutation, the day he arrived here. 'And – he who touches it only casually, as you put it?'

Shilaat gestured. 'He is burned. There are some here with dark scars from rocklight burns.'

'Um. Have those burned ever had children, later?'

'I don't – yes. Yes, of course. Why?'

Cleve shook his head. This was a world different from Earth. On this world, in its system or its galaxy or in this area of space, certain 'natural' laws differed. Here, sorcery existed, if he was to believe the man called Gordon who had sent him here. Here, there was a radioactive *something* within this mountain that glowed, like radium. And burned, but only on contact. Yet it did not sterilize. Here, Robert Cleve realized, he could not rely as solely on Aristotelian logic as he had on Earth. On Earth A was A. Contradictions did not exist. Sometimes they seemed to, but one had only to investigate to learn that they did not. If A equaled B, and B equaled C, then C was equal to A. Here . . . His face writhed in a little smile. He was reminded of an old Earthside song: 'It ain't necessarily so . . .'

Yes. On Earth, things followed, logically; if this was so, then that was necessarily so, despite the song. Here – well here on Andor the song applied.

'I wonder if water boils at a hundred degrees centigrade,' he muttered, 'or freezes, or flies, or turns orange, or just lies there?'

'What did you say, Cleve?'

He shook his head again. 'Sorry, Shilaat. I was muttering. It seemed such a good idea, being able to carry the rocklight about, to light caverns where there is no rocklight. The passage leading here, to your home, for instance. All those torches – constant excursions out through the river and into the jungle, just to get wood to provide light in dark tunnels and passages. Then it must be laid aside to dry after being brought down through the water!'

Shilaat nodded with a whimsical smile. 'Life is seldom easy, Cleve of Earth.'

Cleve gazed at him. Slowly, he pronounced the Adorite word for 'yes' and 'all right' and 'OK'. Pai, Pai, you're right, Shilaat. Does it burn fish skin or llico hide?'

'Pai. We, too, have thought of that.'

'What about wood or rock?'

The rocklight burns neither,' Shilaat said.

'Any effect at all?'

'Not that we are aware of.'

'Hm. Interesting stuff. It glows. It burns selectively – it attacks the kingdoms of animal and vegetable, but apparently not mineral. Of course we can't *prove* it has no effect on the vegetable world, not without experimentation. And perhaps some instruments.

'What sort of instruments, Cleve?'

Cleve chuckled. 'Instruments we aren't about to have access to!' he said. 'You wouldn't believe how far away they are, Shilaat. Um. Shilaat – the white fur. That long, silky stuff you're sitting on. I sleep on it and Siraa has a breech-clout made of it. What is it? Some sort of aquatic animal?'

It was Shilaat's turn to chuckle at ignorance. 'We get it from the Oridorns,' he said.

'But then—'

'They get it from the Orimors,' Shilaat said.

Cleve grinned. 'Should I ask?'

'But you do not understand, my friend. The Oridorns

are at war with Orimora. The Orimors are constantly striving to gain access to Oridorn. To warmth. The Oridorns fight them off – without that rocklight weapon of theirs they would have been exterminated long ago, and it is we who would be fighting off the Orimors.'

Cleve nodded. 'Imperialism,' he said. 'At least it's based on a sensible motive – warmth! I believe that may be unique . . . no. I suppose not. Anyhow, the white fur—'

'As I said, the Oridorns get it from the Orimors. From their bodies. The ones they kill in the Orimor invasions – the Orimors are covered with fur, Cleve, as protection against the not-warmth of their home.' Cleve had told Shilaat the word for 'cold' forgotten in Orisana for lack of necessity; Shilaat had forgotten it again.

'Yes,' Cleve said, 'but my question is—' He stopped. 'You mean that fur is . . . Orimor pelt?'

'Of course,' Shilaat smiled. 'Look at yourself. When man left the water and the caverns and sought to exist in the Overworld – none knows why – he found himself menaced by that great ball of fire in the ceiling, I mean, "sky." He no longer had need of swimming. So – look at yourself. Your skin darkened. Partially burned by the sun, and partially it darkened naturally, I suppose, so you could better stand that sun. You lost the webbing between your toes. I cannot explain your hair – perhaps that, too, darkened because of the sun. And your eyes – perhaps colored eyes can better withstand the light?'

Cleve was staring at him. 'You think – you're saying life began here? Orisana is the birthplace of humans of Andor?'

'Not necessarily Orisana.' Shilaat shrugged. 'But Orisans, yes. What other explanation is there?'

Cleve now knew why his mentioning Orisans' evolving fins and pale skins to Zivaat had shocked and angered him; why Zivaat had warned him not to repeat that heresy to Shilaat! The Orisans, buried within the mountain, interpreted the world in terms of themselves!

Naturally. There was nothing new in that. It was logical – subjectively logical. Cleve said nothing, letting his expression show no surprise or disagreement.

'You are accepted here, Cleve. Certainly there is one among us who is willing to be your mate. Will you stay, now?'

Cleve shook his head. 'I must go, Shilaat,' he said, watching the man's eyes. Yes, he'd thought so. Shilaat was delighted. Nothing personal, of course; Shilaat merely wanted Siraa. *Stay here much longer, boy,* Cleve mused, *and you may get yourself assassinated!*

True enough, but he would not have guessed at the identity of the would-be assassin, or at least, would-be crippler. Not until the strange, eyeless woman from Oridorn told him.

She found him on another of his solitary thinking-walks. He had talked with Shilaat, and with Zivaat, and they had understood, or professed to, and he was 'allowed' to wander without escort, although he was certain Zivaat or someone else was watching where he went.

She came upon him very quietly, the white-skinned, eyeless slave with hair almost transparent. He was sitting on the same rock he'd rested upon to think, that other time he'd wanted solitude, to be alone with his tumultuous mind.

'Cleve?' Her voice was soft; her mouth remained open after she'd spoken.

He nodded. 'Yes. How did you know?'

She advanced a couple of paces to stand just before him. 'I knew. Or thought I knew.'

'And how did you come here so silently?'

'We know where we are and where we are going. We . . . hear. It is what you call "see." We "see" within our heads.' Her mouth moved precisely in that strangely impassive face. Her hands were still; her people did not gesture.

'Um. I apologize – I met two Oridorns both at once, and I don't know whether you are Gaise or Jaire.'

'I am Jaire. We can talk?'

'I'd love to talk with you, Jaire.'

She stood before him in the long, shapeless shift they put on their slaves, her head facing him just as if she were watching him, with only two smooth depressions on either side of the bridge of her nose, where her eyes should be. Her arms hung straight and motionless at her sides. Her mouth, as always, was slightly open.

'You do not plan to stay in Orisana, Cleve of Earth?'

'No. I must either go through the caverns into the water and thus into the jungle, or up through your land.'

'You must go up through Oridorna,' she said, 'and quickly. Or you will die, or worse.'

He did not ask; he could think of many fates worse than death, although the traditional one that matched the cliché had never struck him as such. Perhaps, he had tried to tell himself, it was because he was not a woman. Yet every psychologist who bothered to write, reported that the most frequent phantasy of women was to be fate-worse-than-death.

'Why do you tell me this, Jaire of Oridorna?'

A little shrug: 'I would bargain. You have said that you would leave. I merely want to influence the direction. Shilaat wants you to leave – he is fond of you, but is consumed with desire for Siraa, and will kill you if you stay. Bavuraat, though who also desires her and does not know of Shilaat's infatuations, wants you neither to stay nor to be allowed to go. He will kill you, soon. And – it seems Siraa is determined that you will not leave her. She will do something to you, to cripple you so that you must stay. Failing that, she will kill you rather than have you leave her. It will cause her to lose face, your leaving.'

That last sentence was not much to aid a man's ego, but Cleve did not notice. His ego had never needed boosting, so that he seldom bragged and never bothered to demean others. His mind was struck with the content of her whole statement: so much plotting! He'd had no idea! Three people ready to kill or maim him, and he with no notion of it, other than his faint suspicion of Shilaat – whom he knew would wait, certain Cleve was indeed leaving.

But Siraa! – and Bavuraat!

He bent toward her. 'How does a slave in the household of Shilaat of Orisana know these things, Jaire?'

'We slaves know most of what there is to know. People talk in front of us as if we did not exist, or as if we were animals. Believe what I have told you.' Her face remained impassive.

'That's hard, Jaire. Because you want me to go up into Oridorna, and take you with me.'

Had she had eyes they would have gone very wide, as her mouth did, with a hissing intake of breath. Her hands clutched each other comfortingly. 'How did you know?'

He shrugged, remembering as he did that the gesture was wasted on her. Never mind; on Earth he had gestured and smiled and shrugged while talking on the telephone. It was habit, not demonstration.

'I am not stupid, Jaire of Oridorna. You said that you would bargain, and that you wanted to influence the direction. Why? So that I would take you with me, naturally.'

'She said, 'Yes. I can show you the way, and guarantee your safety among my people. Perhaps we can persuade Zaide to give you a rocklight projector.'

'Who is Zaide?'

These people neither shrugged nor nodded nor gestured as they spoke; they had never seen anyone do so, and thus spoke solely with their mouths. It was strange, disconcerting, almost eerie; a little like conversing with a zombie or a robot. 'Zaide is the Keeper of the Rocklight,' she said simply, and Cleve knew from her tone that Zaide's was a revered post.

He thought about it while she stood silently before him, clad in a long purple gown that would have been reserved for royalty, on Earth at this cultural level. Here purple was not so hard to come by; one did not have to dive for it off the coast of Tyre. He wanted to leave. One way was, apparently, as dangerous as the other. Her way was the unknown, true, but Robert Cleve had never much feared the unknown; it represented a challenge.

Perhaps, as she said, he could obtain one of the projectors with which the Oridorns defended themselves against the Orimors. That should enable him to get past the Orimors, assuming he could clothe himself against the mountaintop cold. It mightn't be pleasant, wearing clothing he knew was made from the pelt of men, or near-men. If it kept him alive, though, he would not turn shuddering from it.

Why not? He was going on anyhow. Why not her way?

'How, Jaire? When?'

'You need only follow me. I know when someone is moving, but I might walk quite close to a stationary person without knowing he was there, against a very rough wall or among rocks. I know only that something is there, not whether it is alive. Thus you would be my eyes, so that we could be sure none saw us. I know the way. We would go while they sleep, of course, so that we could leave more easily and there would be less chance of our being seen.'

'Just like that,' Cleve said. 'No violence?'

'Of course not. There will be no need. Once we are within the passage I know of, there will be none to see us. When we are in darkness, *I* will be *your* eyes.'

He was on the point of feeling remorse about leaving with Shilaat's property – Jaire – when he remembered: She had corroborated the man's intent to kill him if he did not leave, and that soon. Assuming, of course, that she could be believed. *At least partially*, Cleve thought.

'All right, Jaire. Let's make our plan, then.'

Sinuous in the foot-length purple robe, Jaire squatted before him and began to talk quietly and earnestly.

A few feet away, around a corner of the passage, a man with five concentric blue circles on his belly and a single blue stripe between his brows strained to hear. Bavuraat nodded, smiling.

'What will you do when I am gone, Siraa?' Cleve asked.

The mermaid of Orisana came quickly from her back to a sitting position, propping her lithe white body up with her hands behind her.

'You are going?'

'You know I am leaving, Siraa. I have always said so, I have never said otherwise.'

'When?'

Careful, Cleve told himself. *If what Jaire said is true, don't give the pretty schemer a reason to do whatever she intends to do to keep you here!*

'Oh, I am in no hurry,' he said, thinking that a lie was

quite excusable under the circumstances. 'Not for a good while yet.' That was properly vague, not even a lie. How long is 'a good while'?

'I shall miss you,' she said. 'I love your warmth,' She twisted, gazing intensely into his eyes. 'I love you, Cleve.'

He shook his head. 'I don't think so. You love that warmth you mention, and you love my difference, and you love receiving attention because the others know about us.'

She tossed her head so that her long pale hair swished. 'I received plenty of attention before you came,' she said, with more than a little feminine hauteur. 'I am beautiful, and desirable.'

'Yes,' he said, putting out a hand to touch her cheek. She raised hers to hold it against her face.

'But you are wrong, Cleve. I love you. Stay here with me. Stay here and love me, warm me. And let us see if our children are warm like you.'

'I rather doubt there'd be children,' he told her, wondering.

'Why not? Do you think I am not a woman?' Pride again, and hauteur, her chin up.

She doesn't need me to warm her, he thought. *She needs someone of her own kind to tame her, before her uppity ways get her into trouble in a society that places little value on women! I wonder if Shilaat will tame her – or if she will enslave him?*

'I think that we might not have children because we are different,' he told her. 'Has an Oridorn ever borne an Orisan child? Or an Orisan woman an Oridorn child?'

She looked horrified. 'Of course not! But that is completely different. They are inferior creatures. None would want to mate with them. You are . . . different, but you are just like us. It is not your fault that your toes are so strangely naked, disconnected. And I like the color in your eyes and hair and skin.'

'Thank you,' he said, thinking it was, very literally, mighty white of her! 'Uh – I asked what you'd do, though, when I am gone. You wouldn't try to hold me, would you?'

He saw it in her eyes, even as she clutched him and said,

oh no, not if that was what he wanted, returning to that terrible world Outside. But her eyes said Yes – *I shall keep you here, whether you want to remain or not!* And pride spoke as much as – according to her – love. It was as he had said: She would miss the attention, and the novelty of warmth. She had probably done some bragging, put on some airs with the other women here. She would lose face when he left; they would say he had abandoned her, that Siraa could not hold the man she wanted. Cleve felt sorry for her – but not enough to stay, or to trust her. And he did not love her, although he had no desire to hurt the woman who had saved his life.

'Shilaat desires you,' he said.

The head tossed again; white hair swished and swirled again on her shoulders. 'Shilaat eats like a Treeman. Shilaat is growing fat and losing his hair.'

'Oh come now, Siraa. He is ruler of Orisana. You will be first among the women of Orisana!'

He saw that got to her, and thus he felt less remorse when he arose later, while she slept, and crept out to where he was to meet Jaire of Oridorna. He knew that he would not see Siraa of Orisana again, and he knew they would both be far better off. But he felt more a man for the experience of having known her.

Chapter Thirteen

The Tunnel to Oridorna

They were almost in darkness, just rounding a turn in the narrow corridor that put them beyond the last area of luminescence in the wall, when Jaire halted. She touched the arm of the other woman, Gaise; they had appeared together, and certainly Cleve could not send Gaise back.

'What is it?' he whispered, watching as they turned to face back the way they'd come, still as statues made of albaster and robed in purple. Their mouths were open. Jaire replied in a whisper, without moving her alertly held head.

'We are followed. The fact that we have not heard them proves that they come stealthily. Also slowly.'

'Then let's go,' he said, 'and faster.'

She went on, with Gaise close behind her and Cleve following Gaise. To them, there was no difference; to Cleve, their way led into increasing darkness. Seeing a hand-sized rock lying loose against the cavern wall, he bent. Just as he picked it up there was a loud scraping clank of metal behind them. The two Oridorn women halted, spinning about to stand as if frozen. 'Seeing,' he knew; focusing their radar sense or whatever it was that enabled them to walk so surely, to set down plates without banging the table, to know how close a wall or a table or another person was.

Behind them there was absolute silence.

'They have stopped,' Gaise whispered.

Just as she did, the shout bellowed out behind them, echoing along the narrow tunnel in the mountain like the hollow voice of a ghost.

'Cleve! We know you're there, and we know you're fleeing to Oridorna with two slaves! You were more than welcome to leave – but not as a thief! Come back, all three of you – we have swords, and you're unarmed.'

'Their arms are too long,' Jaire said, very intent. 'Yes – they carry swords.'

'How far,' Cleve asked, 'to the shaft leading up to Oridorna?'

'Not much farther, but—'

'Run,' he told them, 'or go as fast as you can. I'll be right behind you. If they overtake us, I'll try to stop them. This tunnel is too narrow for them to come at me two abreast.' He turned back toward the unseen pursuers.

'Bavuraat? Go back and let me be – I've a sword and you can come at me only one at a time. I've little to lose – I know of your plan to murder me!'

He looked about for more rocks. The Oridorns were already fleeing noiselessly up the passage, nearly running. Without waiting for Bavuraat's reply, Cleve turned and followed. A few paces farther on, he stumbled, grunting as he hurt his knee, but picking up the stone that had tripped him. While the two women were making incredibly good time, considering their sightlessness, they were far from running. Bavuraat and his men should have no trouble overtaking them. The bobbing, flickering light told Cleve they had a torch, and were following. Their feet slapped as they came; they were trotting, the fastest safe speed possible in this narrow, irregular, twisting, and rock-strewn cavern.

He ran into Gaise.

'This is the place,' Jaire said excitedly, panting a little. 'We must climb.

The tunnel ended in an apparent cul-de-sac. But its terminal wall led upward, through a dark shaft. To Oridorna. She began to climb up the blank end of the passage, crying out to those who might be above.

Cleve alternated watching her assent – closely, too closely followed by Gaise – with looking back down the passage at the sounds of shouts and approaching feet. These were accompanied by the light of the torch carried by one of the pursuers.

Now Gaise's legs were higher than his face; Jaire had vanished up into the darkness. For him to climb as they did, in total darkness, would be hard enough under any circumstances. With armed men leaping up after him, hurling torches or spears or swords – he knew it was impossible.

For the second time on Andor, Cleve prepared to die.

Now he could see the torch itself, and the men, and the glitter of their blades in the torchlight. He looked up.

Gaise, too, had disappeared into the blackness, clambering up the wall. Both Oridorn women were still shouting:

'Oridorns! Oridorns! Help!'

Cleve sighted on the torch, striving to land his hurled stone just below it and to its left; he assumed its carrier held it in his left hand, with his weapon in his right. Hurling the stone with all his strength, Cleve quickly transferred another from his left hand to his right. Again he aimed and threw, then bent for the pitifully few more stones he had accumulated as they hurried along.

There was a yell, then a clatter as the rock rebounded from its target and rolled. The torch appeared to stagger. Cleve heard a loud curse and the sound of a falling body. Not the torchbearer; someone else must have slipped on the rolling stone. The second stone missed, somehow, clattering.

Cleve launched a third and a fourth missile in quick succession, bending instantly for more.

There was the high-pitched, hideous sound of a man's agonized scream. And a groan, in another voice. A sword clanged and clattered as its owner went down. Cleve wondered where his missile had hit the man who had shrieked and fallen, dropping his blade. In the face? The eye? The groin? Or more prosaically, the leg? The fourth stone, too, had struck flesh, eliciting a groan. All he had to do was get them there. They might possibly go over their heads, but the pursuers were too closely crowded in the narrow passage for a stone to go past them.

Cleve paused, listening to Bavuraat's voice striving to outyell the others; he told them to string out, one behind the other, hugging the wall. And to advance.

Cleve hefted his last two chunks of rock. He glanced upward.

There was nothing to be seen. The two women had ceased their shouts. The blackness of the shaft had swallowed them.

They've escaped, he thought. *They've escaped slavery and returned to their people. Why yell? Why worry about a man of another race? He's served his purpose!*

He slammed the fifth rock down the tunnel, listened to it strike a wall, then another, then something softer than rock that screamed, then the tunnel floor. He had scored, not so miraculously because of the tunnel's narrowness, several hits. Yet he had no idea as to the seriousness of any of them, nor for that matter how many cries and groans might have come from one highly unfortunate pursuer.

'Throw your brand as hard as you can,' Bavuraat yelled: 'Perhaps it will light him so that we can see him!'

They were now no more than twenty yards away, Cleve gauged, watching the whirling wooden torch impregnated with grease from the llico. It whooshed, loud in the tunnel, as it spun, and as it came rushing toward him, streaming a quivering tail of fire. It struck the floor several feet in front of him in a bright cascade of sparks. It lay there, burning far less brightly for lying on the stone surface.

Keeping close against the wall, Cleve edged toward the torch, until it was only three or four feet away. He had but one remaining stone, and had been unable to find more in the darkness. The torch showed him no more. If he picked it up, he would make of himself a target, for stones or steel.

He hoped the two eyeless slaves – ex-slaves, now – were alive and well in Oridorna. He wished sincerely that the way home had not led him into a cul-de-sac. If he could have kept on moving—

That gave him an idea.

'I can't see him,' a man yelled, 'torch or no torch!'

'I'm not going on until he is out of rocks to throw!' another snarled.

'Go, then,' Bavuraat yelled. 'He has stopped throwing them!'

Cleve flung his last stone. He turned instantly and returned to the rocky wall forming the end of the passage. With his heart feeling as if it were in his mouth, yet threatening to pound its way through his chest, he commenced climbing, slowly and carefully and with trepidation, a wall he could not see – up into a shaft of total blackness.

Behind him the first voice roared, 'He's stopped throwing them? That one barely missed me! I agree – let's wait him out. He can't have an endless supply of rocks! And the torch will show him if he tries to creep on us.'

Good boy, Cleve thought, feeling about until he found a granite projection that, without promising, told him it might consider staying in place while he pulled himself up another few inches.

He was no more than six feet off the cavern floor when his foot slipped and a rock fell noisily and he was just able to save himself from falling back. He succeeded in painfully banging one knee and in scraping an ounce or so of skin off several knuckles.

'He didn't throw that one,' Bavuraat yelled, almost screaming. 'You idiots! He's climbing! He'll escape! *rush* him!'

'YOU rush him, Bav, you're the one so anxious to kill him! Me, I can sleep just as well with him alive as dead!'

'No, you can't,' Bavuraat snapped, and Cleve gained another few inches, gasping. 'Not when I tell Shilaat you let him escape with his two slavegirls!'

Cleve paused, gasping, his arms and clawing fingers already aching, and shouted back: 'Bavuraat will tell Shilaat nothing if you kill him!' And he moved up another two or three inches.

Despair began to nudge hope aside, then, for he heard them coming. They had ignored his suggestion, or it had only angered them; they were running toward him, aided by the torch still flickering weakly on the floor. He had not been so brilliant after all. He'd hoped they would wait long enough, making certain he was out of missiles, to enable him to get himself far up the wall. But climbing in the darkness was no simple matter, and for the second time he realized the advantage, in some situations, of sightlessness – provided the sightless one possessed a built-in radar system enabling him to find his way in the darkness, even to find hand- and footholds!

He should have held to his first idea: to wait there for them, near the torch, then snatch it up to meet their charge. Perhaps that way he'd have got his hand on a sword. This way he'd only get a sword or one of their short spears in the back.

He was about eight feet off the cavern floor when they reached the wall he had climbed. One of them snatched up the torch, waving it. Cleve scrambled, now able to see several tempting handholds above. The shaft remained black overhead.

'Stand back,' Bavuraat said. 'The torch will bring him down! All it has to do is touch him – reflex will make him fall!'

Danger, Cleve thought, *and excitement . . . and perhaps your death, Mr Cleve. Right, Gordon, on all three counts. Good-bye, to you and your scummy organization that promised me at least another man's position and followers! I've never had either. I haven't had even a fighting chance!*

He heard the rope as it rushed by, dropped from above, and he turned his head just in time to see the white male body as it hurtled down the rope; surely the white-haired man was burning his hands!

'An Oridorn!'

'Look out, he—'

Cleve looked down. The eyeless man of Oridorna struck the tunnel floor only a few feet in front of the Orisans; there were four, Cleve saw, in the torchlight. The man yanked something that looked like metal from the belt he wore and held it before him. Cleve saw the flash of the luminescent rocklight, Orisana's best friend.

Not this time. The Orisans screamed. Swords clanged to the rocky floor at their feet. Cleve saw nothing, heard nothing; there was no sound, no visible beam. But they fell, and he knew he was watching an Oridorn rocklight projector in action. An Andorite pistol.

The man raised his head as if looking up at Cleve. 'Take hold of the rope, Cleve of Earth,' he said. 'They will pull you up.'

Cleve's hand closed around the rope, carefully; he'd be

sure he had a safe grip before he let go with his other hand and took his feet from their precarious perches on tiny outcroppings in the shaft wall.

He glanced down. Yelled. The Oridorn was already jerking up the rocklight projector. All too late: Bavuraat lunged up from the floor and spitted the poor fellow on his curved sword, straight through the belly.

Cleve kicked at the wall, swung a little, and let go the rope. He dropped directly onto Bavuraat's back. Both of them fell, and Cleve knew new pain as he slammed to the rocky tunnel floor and rolled. Something cold touched his thigh as he rolled across it.

Steel. Or iron.

He scrambled around, snatching up the sword as he rose. Bavuraat must have been behind one of the others and missed being swept by the invisible ray the Oridorn projected. It was lethal, Cleve realized. The men at his feet were dead, all three of them.

Bavuraat rose, bloody scimitar in hand, and turned, grinning. The smile left his face when he saw that the man facing him was also sword-armed, not defenseless as he'd expected.

'You plotted to kill me, Bavuraat, because you want Siraa,' Cleve told him. 'You followed me like a thief, skulking, and you'd have killed us, all three. Now the man who saved my life is dead at your hands. Come, Bavuraat. Die.'

'How – how did you know I meant to kill you?' Bavuraat demanded, half-crouching.

It was all Cleve wanted to know; Jaire had spoken the truth. And she had sent help. She had neither lied nor escaped to abandon him. And Bavuraat was as she had described him: a skulking killer. Cleve did not wait to be attacked; he leaped at the other man.

Bavuraat's sword came up to meet Cleve's, but Cleve's blade was not there. He twisted as he leaped, swinging the curved sword, and Bavuraat parried empty air.

In midleap, Cleve brought his scimitar sharply down. Not sharply enough; it bit into Bavuraat's arm, and the Orisan cried out, but the cut was not serious and he did not drop his own weapon. They were long blades, too long for the confined space in which they dueled. The curved swords were meant for open fighting, for the world outside this strange, self-contained one within the mountain.

Bavuraat swung and they faced one another, the ghostly white man with the bleeding arm and the darker one with the jet club of hair on his nape, bound by a silver ring. Their eyes met, searing gray ones and icily pale ones like those of a fish. For a moment they were still, panting, two near-naked men in the bowels of a mountain. Their faces, their bodies were lit eerily by the glim lying on the cavern floor a few feet away.

Bavuraat came in a two-step advance, swinging his scimitar in a vicious side-armed delivery. Cleve's sword leaped out to meet the other blade, to parry the hard-swung stroke, and metal clanged loudly and then clanged again and again as it echoed and reechoed along the cavern and in the shaft overhead. After beating Bavuraat's blade aside, Cleve strove to cut, backhand, at the man's chest; the Orisan backed too quickly. Again they gazed at each other in frozen crouches.

Then Cleve advanced, his eyes on Bavuraat's legs, his sword swinging forward low. Bavuraat's blade arced down to intercept the hamstringing cut. And Cleve's biceps sprang up as his arm curved, almost in a cranking motion. His sword shot up as he lunged, and the long, curved blade entered Bavuraat's body just below his sternum. It passed completely through him. He stared at Cleve with very wide eyes, eyes that remained wide and staring as he fell back against the rocky wall, hung there motionless a moment, and then slid slowly down to a sitting position. Cleve withdrew his sword from the corpse.

Chapter Fourteen

The Meat of Oridorna

Cleve glanced up the shaft. It remained dark. The rope hung there, motionless. There was no sound.

He bent quickly over the body of the Oridorn man who'd slid fearlessly down to rescue a man he had never met, a man he could never see. Opening his fingers, Cleve extricated the little object they clutched.

It was not of metal, as it had appeared. It was a box, carefully carved from two, no three pieces of some smooth, bluish stone. His thumb, he supposed, would go into this loop of llicogut. Pull it. That would open the counterbalanced, cleverly hinged little 'door' in one end of the closed box. That, presumably, exposed the rocklight within, somehow channeled outward in an invisible beam that meant death to breathing creatures. It weighed much less than a pound.

Shaking his head, he bent over the Orisans downed by the beam. He turned one over and made a face; the man's chest was blackened, neatly holed as if by a laser beam. There was another burn, another hole in his arm; the Oridorn had downed all three of them by swinging the weapon. All three were dead. Cleve wondered: Had they died of the burns, of the hole that ate swiftly into and through their bodies, or of a burst of pure radioactivity?

He did not know. Nor would he experiment with the little stone box until he knew more of it; it held far too much potential danger for casual experimentation. Again he glanced at the rope hanging from the dark shaft. It twitched. Others were up there, waiting, listening. He called up.

'Jaire? Gaise? I am Cleve of Earth. The Orisans are dead, but Bavuraat slew your man. I will secure your rope to him so that you may pull him up.'

'We will descend to handle that, Cleve of Earth,' a man's

voice said, and the rope writhed as, somewhere up in that absolute darkness, someone swung down on it. Cleve glanced about.

On Bavuraat's belt hung a pouch; it was a hide pouch, worn by the Treemen on their belts for the purpose of carrying arrowheads. Cleve bent swiftly and removed the dead man's belt, transferring it to his own hips. He wore, otherwise, only one of the tight groin pouches of Orisana. As soon as he had secured the belt about himself he emptied the pouch – it contained nothing of consequence – and pushed the Oridorn rocklight projector down into it. The pouch was equipped with a flap closure with two punched holes; it was simply fastened by means of a bit of gut from some jungle animal. Cleve fastened it.

The man who came down the rope was completely naked, save for a baldric he wore, a finger-width strap from left shoulder to right hip. From it depended a flint dagger and, Cleve saw with some amusement, a pouch similar to his own. He had created a holster for the projector; the Oridorns had thought of that long ago!

The man was as Jaire and Gaise and the dead Oridorn near his feet; pale, almost translucent of skin, with that faint bluish cast from the visible veins beneath; stringy white hair that was almost not-white, almost translucent. And he was eyeless, the sockets closed over smoothly with skin, leaving only two little depressions beneath his brow on either side of his nose. Like the women, he had no eyebrows. And his mouth was ajar.

'I am Zaire of Oridorna.'

'I am Cleve of Earth.' Cleve extended his hand. Then, despite the fact that there was none to see his faux pas, he felt embarrassed and hot of face. But as he started to withdraw the hand, Zaire gripped his wrist. His fingers touched Cleve's palm.

'Yes,' he said, 'I see that you are unarmed. Thank you. Jaire and Gaise say that you are neither of the Treeman nor of Orisana, that you are from the outer world and that the Orisans say that there is color in your eyes and your hair, and on your flesh. Is this so?'

'Yes,' he said, 'I am a man like you. Except for the color and my eyes, we are identical.'

'What,' Zaire of Oridorna asked, 'is color?'

Cleve raised his eyebrows. It was an old philosophical question on Earth – how to describe colour to a blind man.

'Without eyes you can perceive distance and size, is that not true?'

'Of course.' It was strange, talking with an erect, almost statue-still man who neither nodded nor gestured and whose stance was as if he were intently staring – save that he had no eyes with which to stare.

'We perceive the same with our eyes, but we are also able to see that the objects differ in color as well as in size. It has nothing to do with shape or texture, Zaire of Oridorna. As a matter of fact – I find it impossible to explain to you, any more than you could describe to me how you knew I had stretched out my hand to you. Nature has given us different abilities. I cannot conceive of not seeing color, you cannot conceive of what color is. Nor light and dark. They are unnecessary to you.'

'Yes. You are not quite right, I think, but that is for later. We want all of them up in Oridorna. You will help me?'

'Of course. But – you mean your people want the bodies of the Orisans your young warrior slew?'

'Yes. How was he killed?'

Cleve told him.

'You were on the rope and had only to call to be drawn up,' Zaire said. 'You were unarmed. But you dropped back down here to fight the Orisan. Why?

Cleve cocked his head; a tiny smile pulled at the corner of his mouth. 'It was my fight. The Oridorn saved me, and died for me. I – did not think about it. I avenged him.'

'It was not your fight,' Zaire said. 'You rescued my sister and another of our women, stolen and enslaved by the Orisans. You are a brave man, Cleve of Earth. You have the deathbox he carried?'

Cleve had intended to lie, or had thought he would. He could not. 'Yes,' he said.

'Keep it,' Zaire told him. 'It is yours. You are a warrior of

Oridorna. Come – we will let our dead warrior be drawn up first.'

They did, working together, Zaire's 'sight' nearly as good as Cleve's. Once, twice, five times the rope went up and returned. Then a sixth time: in the basket lowered from above, Cleve heaped the Orisan weapons and watched them vanish upward into blackness. Again the rope descended, and Cleve, standing alone, felt a qualm as he watched Zaire drawn up. He had known considerable violence and treachery since his arrival on this planet. Again he felt doubt; suppose the rope did not return for him? The Oridorns had their slaves back – one of them Zaire's sister – and their dead warrior and four Orisans and all their arms. Zaire had warned Cleve to bring the torch, but—

– the rope dropped, whipping snakelike in the shaft. Clutching the torch in his left hand, Cleve wrapped the rope twice about his right wrist and gripped its end. It would not be comfortable, being pulled up a shaft by one arm for an unknown distance, but – there was no light in Oridorna. It was not needed.

'Pull,' he called, and he was pulled.

His fingers and his arm and his shoulder and pectoral muscles ached by the time he felt a hand touch, then grip his right wrist; he had no way of knowing just how long that slender shaft was, but it was very deep indeed.

He found himself surrounded by eyeless, naked people. The women – except for the two purple-clad girls who came forward and knelt at his feet – wore nothing. The men wore baldrics like Zaire's, and hewing or stabbing weapons of various sizes and descriptions. Many wore the little pouch he assumed held the rocklight projector – 'deathbox,' Zaire had called it; 'sidsorn': 'sid' ('death'), plus 'sorn' ('small chest for storing valuables'). Others did not; either they were short on the awful weapons or they were carried only by a select few.

'This is Cleve of Earth,' Zaire said, in a loud voice, turning as he spoke so that none would miss his words. 'He is of the outer world, though neither an Orimor nor a Treeman. He was a captive of the Orisans, although they did not enslave him. He has returned to us Baise-daughter Gaise and my sister Jaire, whom the Orisans enslaved. They were the personal property of Silaat of Orisana and served at his table!'

The gathering of eyeless people murmured, and Cleve wondered at the two women's station among them.

'Though he could have been pulled up, he returned, unarmed, to slay the man who killed Vaine. He is a brave man, and truthful, and our friend. I have given him Vaine's deathbox, and I recognize him as a warrior of Oridorna.' He turned to Cleve.

'My sister and Baise-daughter Gaise still kneel at your feet, Cleve of Earth. Do you free them?'

'I – free them?' Then Cleve realized; he had saved both of them. Not from death, perhaps, but from the living one of slavery. 'I release you from death, both of you,' he said, taking a hand of each Oridorn and helping her to her feet. They stood before him a moment, facing him. Then Gaise turned and rushed to a man and woman standing nearby, both with seamed old faces. The trio clasped each other.

Zaire wrapped his arm around his sister. 'Come, Cleve,' he said, and followed them. They went surely through the darkness, he following with the torch. It was pitiful, this land of Oridorna within the mountain. He had thought there was little that was civilized or beautiful about the Orisan existence; they were glorified cavemen. Here was less glory. The Oridorns lived in utter darkness. They wore no clothing: it was needed neither for warmth nor walls. The paper-colored people moved like ghosts through the dark, their mouths slightly open.

He soon learned that they did possess art: It dealt in textures, and he was barely able to appreciate it, with his eyes open, or as an experiment, closed. They were a courtly, quiet people, too, far removed from the cavemen of Earth's misty past. Cleve felt depressed among them, sad. They were locked here forever, with exits only above and below them, and those exits were closed to them by deadly enemies. Even with the deathboxes, the Oridorns would never win their way down into Orisana; an armed man had but to stand still and wait for one to come near, and to kill him. A few of the deathboxes in the hands of the people below – and Oridorna and the Oridorns would vanish forever, wiped out in what might be called a genocidal mercy killing.

They were human beings, and they were calm, and quiet, and unhurried. And they were happy. Never having had sight, never having been sightless people among seeings ones, they did not miss the eyes denied them from birth. And they 'saw,' both with their fingers and with the other sense with which they had been provided as compensation for their unneeded eyes. Dwellers in eternal darkness, they were one of nature's strangest creations.

Once the world outside learns of them, Cleve thought, *they will never be the same. Man cannot stand to leave something such as this alone.*

He vowed silently that none would ever know of Oridorna from his lips.

He repeated the vow aloud, as he sat with Jaire and her brother and their grandfather, an ancient man named Zaide. Their father had died in a battle with the Orisans, a few months before Jaire's birth. Their mother had remarried and died, two years ago. Jaire was sad, without the relief of tears; she had been captured by Orisana three years ago, and thus returned to find that she would never know her mother again.

'Thank you, Cleve,' Zaire said. 'I believe you. A man who would admit to having a deathbox when he could have lied would not lie to me now. I believe that Cleve of Earth will not reveal our existence to the outer world, although we do not fear it and its people. You are our first contact with it, aside from the Orimors, who do indeed live outside. If all are as you—'

'Don't place me on a pedestal,' Cleve told him in some embarrassment. 'I have killed. I will lie if I must, I have no doubt, although I have not found it necessary yet. But – all those Outside are not as I am. You say you do not fear the outer world, Zaire. Do.'

'There are things we must tell you,' Zaire said.

Cleve looked up as a woman entered with their supper; she was Jaire's aunt, the sister of her mother. Her husband had died, and she had moved back to this cavern of the old man Zaide, the Keeper of the Rocklight.

'After we eat,' Cleve said, 'or as we eat. Pardon me, but the food is here – and I am famished.'

Zaire's hand came over to touch his wrist, then grip it. 'No, my friend Cleve. Before we eat. Listen. We take no slaves, as do our enemies, both above and below. We have never attacked them, we fight only to defend ourselves. Within these caverns we have vast quantities of the mushrooms you ate below, in Orisana, save that here they are much thicker and grow to far greater size. We have no fish, no llicos. No animals. As you know, the people of Orisana have weapons they take from the Treemen, and fish and animals and wood they can obtain by leaving their land through the water. Too, they have slaves from both the Treemen and from us, as well as swords, also taken from us. In our turn, while we take no slaves, we have obtained minute quantities of fish from the Orisans we have been forced to kill, and tools and gut and hide. The swords of Orisana – these come from us, but we have them from the Orimors – who have them from some other peoples, Outside.'

Frowning, Cleve nodded, automatically. He knew that even were he to spend the rest of his life with these sightless people he would never cease nodding, shrugging, gesturing; making all the visual aids to speech that served all men in all places. Except in Oridorna.

'I understand all that, Zaire.'

'Pai,' Zaire said; he prefaced many utterances with the Andorite affirmative word. 'But I have not done. Could you live without meat?'

'I suppose so. Many people have, and do, although I have never tried.' Cleve eyed the savory meat on the stone plate before him, though it was uncooked, he thought he'd have no difficulty getting it down. He had tasted meat but once since he came with Siraa from the river.

'Yes – let me put it this way, then,' Zaire said. 'We have found that we cannot survive on mushrooms alone. We sicken and die.'

'I can understand that.' Cleve looked around at them. All

of them, Zaire and Jaire and the old man Zaide and the aunt – all of them sat stiff and attentive. He could not be sure, for these people were nigh-expressionless, but they seemed to be worried, apprehensive. 'Man needs more than a diet of mushrooms for survival.'

'Yes. I am glad you understand, Cleve. The Orisans and the Orimors do not. We know this from those few we have captured – they were horrified, and we were sorry to have to decide we could not let them go back to their people. Thus, we have told no one in centuries. When I say "we" I am speaking of my people historically, you understand, not necessarily about this body.' Zaire struck his bare chest with a closed fist.

Cleve waited. There had to be more. Zaire wanted to tell him; he had initiated this one-sided conversation. Cleve saw no need to prompt him. He had always been thus, on Earth as on Andor. Gordon had noticed it immediately, that perceptive man now so far away.

'We have no meat,' Zaire said. 'There is no animal life in Oridorna, and we cannot gain the Outside to hunt, as the Orisans and the Orimors do.'

'I see . . .' Cleve saw without seeing.

'But we must have meat.'

Cleve gazed down at the meat on his plate. The Oridorns must have meat to survive. They could not; there were no animals here, and they had access to none. But – here he sat at table with them – figuratively speaking; each of them had an individual stone that served as a private table. Before him was meat, savory and fresh. Uncooked, true, but rich, nourishing meat. Flesh.

He stared at it. Raised his head to look at them, one by one. Looked down again at his plate. He was sure he knew the answer, but he did not want to believe it. Centuries of custom, of taboo, rebelled in his brain. No!

'What – what is this on my plate, Zaire?'

Zaire sighed. 'Meat. Cleve. That which is necessary to our survival, to the survival of a people kept locked up here by their enemies.'

'What is this on my plate, Zaire?'

'Meat, Cleve of Earth. The flesh of the men you and I secured to the rope to be brought up here to my waiting people.'

Cleve shot to his feet, staring about at them.

Cannibals! Like the Treemen, they were eaters of human flesh! Somehow – somehow it was even worse that the flesh was not cooked, that it had been hacked raw and dripping from the bodies of the men he and that Oridorn warrior had slain, and served up to them, minutes later – still warm.

'Which of you is eating the body of your lately slain country man?' he demanded.

'None of us,' Zaire said quietly. 'That is his family's privilege. It would not be right for—'

But Cleve, his stomach churning, his brain reeling, was already striding away from his new friends and their ghoulish meal.

Chapter Fifteen

The Keeper of the Rocklight

Cleve had lain long alone, watching the torch burn down, thinking. He did not know where he was, who belonged to this little cavern that became a pocket forming a ten-by-ten room with a thirty-foot ceiling. None seemed to claim it; none stopped him as he strode past feasting Oridorns – who looked up at his passing, parted lips quivering, as if following him with the eyes they did not possess. He had walked long and far, and had turned into this side tunnel and found himself in this stony room with a pile of white, silken-soft pelts on the floor.

He had lain long alone, and he had turned it over and over in his mind. It was – ecology.

The pelts he lay upon, shielding his body from reposing on solid granite – the silken fur came from men, or near-men, the Orimors. Apparently they raided some peoples living lower down the mountain, or at its foot; from them they took scimitars and food. Too, animals abode in the mountains, also providing food for them. Their pelts were their natural compensation for their climate; without them they could not have survived atop the mountain. The pelts in turn provided both garb and comfort for the other peoples, the Orisans and the Oridorns, who had access to no animals. True, the Orisans did. But they were in deadly danger when they left their cavern – in darkness, always in darkness, for the warning sun was death to a race of albinos. The swords, passed down in combat from one level to the next, enabled the Orisans better to cope with the savage Treemen and the occasional animals they met Outside.

Without attempting to, they provided the Oridorns with the fruits of their forays; rope and bones and fish skin with llico and tentacles, and pouches for the Oridorn weapons – pouches taken from the Treemen.

It was what is called a balanced ecology, using the term only slightly different from the biologists' intent.

But there was a flaw in it. The Oridorns, like all creatures everywhere, must fight for survival. And they must have meat. But – there was no meat available to them. And their mushrooms provided no protein.

Nor, Cleve told himself, was there meat available *according to Earthside taboos.* Yet of course there was meat. Man did what was necessary; there was no physical, no biological reason for him not to eat the flesh of man. To the Oridorns locked within the mountain it was necessary: They ate. And they survived.

Learning, ages ago, that this was a strong taboo among other peoples, his Oridorn host had felt compelled to explain to Cleve, and warn him. Zaire had not had to do so; they could have allowed their guest to eat his fill. They could have told him later. Or they might never have told him. Cleve wondered if he would ever have known, were it not for Zaire's honesty and consideration.

He watched the flickering ghost patterns from his torch as they danced and writhed on the ceiling. He lay on his back, staring, his hands behind his head.

These were probably the most moral people he had ever encountered. They believed in honesty, and practiced it despite its consequences. Surrounded by slave takers, they took no slaves. Surrounded by fiercely warlike people, they fought only in defense. They accepted a stranger – a very different stranger – without question. They were totally honest, he mused rather bitterly, *to a fault! He didn't have to tell me, damn him!*

But they broke a taboo, a part of the moral code of nearly every people on Cleve's planet, and apparently, on this one.

Because they had to, they ate human flesh.

Perhaps they did not have to, and there were some who might well say so. They could die.

A vegetarian cast into the desert with a cow or a goat – would he eat the animal, breaking his code, or die?

Well, Cleve told himself, *he might die. But that isn't a true analog, not a fair one. That man is a fanatic, one man alone with a personal belief different from others'. These people are members of the race of man, however different. Their choice is simple.*

Eat of the flesh of thine enemy, or die.

Thine enemy's flesh? Somewhere, somewhere in this collection of unlit caves and stone corridors and tunnels called Oridorna, a family sat together, eating a member of that family. He had been someone's son, someone's grandson, someone's brother; perhaps also husband and father. Was that no different? This was not merely – 'merely' – eating the dead enemy to survive. This was – monstrous.

Cleve gave the ceiling a rueful smile. Monstrous? No, it was obviously a part of their society, a ritual. Eating him, Zaire had said was 'his family's privilege. It would not be right for' *others* – Cleve finished the sentence – *to eat him.* That must be approximately what Zaire said, or would have said, as his guest stalked away from his board.

The family privilege. With honor, Cleve mused; with honor and ceremony, no doubt, and in peace they eat the body of their beloved son. In whom, doubtless, they were well pleased.

True, he'd known people who practiced cannibalism once weekly, sometimes more often, in concert, in a ceremonial rite. They might not have done so had their repast been warm flesh rather than a thin wafer of white dough!

Yes, he thought. *And I did not believe, and I stayed well away from such ceremonies. But I did not turn from them in disgust! Autres temps, autres moeurs* – other times, other customs. Yes, and other places, too, have customs differing from one's own. The men of Europe, kissing one another, in an act totally unacceptable among Americans, so nervous of their manhood; the men of India, eschewing beef, even unto starvation, so that once three millions died in a single bad season – surrounded by cattle; the men of the Arabic lands, belching as loudly as possible and never touching their food with one hand, the one reserved for wiping themselves; on and on.

One may either accept these customs, he mused, *or reject them. But what could be more childish than to express dis-*

gust at the customs of other people? One can either be a human, a civilized being, or one can be a missionary, expressing disgust at a happy people's natural nudity and swiftly teaching them about clothing and guilt – while incidentally, infecting them with venereal disease and pointing out to them what promiscuity is, and divorce.

The women of ancient religions, called 'temple harlots' by Christians, had as much right to call Christians 'cannibals.'

You are a child, he told himself. *You have insulted a good people, who were honorable enough to warn you of their custom, a custom necessary to their survival as individuals and as a people.*

I am a warrior,' he replied to his own small and not-so-still inner voice. *I have always been a warrior, an atavist, on Earth and on Andor. I am not a sociologist, trained to accept other customs, other mores, no matter what form they take.*

Cleve sighed. He would go back, and he would apologize, and he would eat – mushrooms.

Starting to roll over to get up, he realized: Go back? He had no notion of the way back! He had merely wandered. He did not know where he was, and had no idea how to return to where he'd been. He was lost.

'Cleve?'

Her voice was soft, as all their voices were soft, and sad, as he had made it sad. She had doffed the hated purple robe, a symbol of her servitude in Orisana. She stood before him as all her people stood, clothed only in dignity and honor and the clothing provided by her Creator.

I did not rebel at that, he told himself angrily. *I accepted their nudity with no qualm, no problem. What is it in us men that so horrifies us at the notion of eating the meat of one particular animal, the beast called man?*

'Jaire?'

'I—'

'Don't say it. Don't say anything. I must apologize to your family.' He rose, and she came quickly to him, against him, a woman like other women, different as Siraa was different, and yet different again from Siraa, for Jaire possessed no eyes and no vanity. She held herself tight against him, her face against his chest.

'It is as they said in Orisana,' she said, her voice muffled, her lips soft and tickly as they moved against his bare chest. 'You are so warm! No wonder Siraa wanted to keep you always with her! No wonder the others were jealous and spiteful!'

He touched her hair, like silk, nearly transparent silk. Were they, Jaire?'

'Oh, yes. She bragged, bragged of your warmth and your attention, and she flaunted her having won you. They were jealous, all of them, and spiteful to her. She is paying now, I suppose – they will be even more cruel, but now she is defenseless.'

He sighed. 'No, Jaire, a woman is never defenseless,' he said, realizing that Jaire was indeed a woman, soft and shapely, her body a caress against his, and that he was indeed a man, no matter how differently made or colored. 'Besides, she will be Shilaat's mate, first woman in Orisana.'

'Yes,' Jaire whispered against him; she still clung.

He wrapped his hands around her chill arms. 'Take me back to them, Jaire,' he said. 'Take me back so that I may apologize, and then eat – I am starved.'

'What will you eat?'

'Mushrooms,' he said. 'Mushrooms.'

He followed her back, her hand cool in his, wondering what it was like to be naturally so cool of flesh and body, and then to feel someone who radiated warmth. He had no frame of reference; he had been impressed with the heat of feverish persons – it was pleasant at times, strangely so. But it had not been a genuinely or generally pleasant sensation, because it was not purely physical. His mind had been involved: His reaction to that almost-burning warmth had been colored by his knowledge that this person was sick.

Robert Cleve's father had died, twisting, sweating, his temperature past 44 Centigrade, with his son standing by the bed, holding the hand his father clutched and squeezed.

Jaire moved slowly through the dark labyrinth, and again they passed among her people, and entered the side cavern that led to the home of her family, and again he faced those attentive, eyeless faces. They sat as he had left them, save that now there were no plates on the flat little stone table before each of them. Each head was erect, almost tilted in parted-lip alertness as their Oridorn sixth sense 'listened' or 'felt' or 'saw' his approach with Jaire.

'I am sorry,' he said simply. 'As you know, people outside Oridorna do not eat human flesh. For some reason it is a very severe breach of our code. I admit I do not even know why. I understand its necessity to you, and I apologize for my irrational and unfriendly reaction. I have insulted friends and hosts.'

'I will prepare your plate,' Jaire said, and went away into the other pocket in the stone that served them as kitchen.

Cleve had nearly forgotten; he offered apology and invited challenge and invective; they rejected the offer all around, telling him that barbarous Outside custom did not prevail in Oridorna. Cleve ate. The mushrooms of Oridorna, like those smaller ones of Orisana, tasted like old bread; he was hungry, and he ate.

'The post of Keeper of the Rocklight, Keeper Zaide, is it a hereditary one?'

The old man nodded. 'Yes, Cleve of Earth, and call me Zaide, here among the family. I have learned this thing called nodding, you see.'

'I do see,' Cleve said, 'I was trying to decide whether to ask you or not. The message is clear: You have learned some of the customs of my people, I must learn and be tolerant of yours.' And his stomach lurched, and he fought there among the family of Jaire and Zaire a harder battle than he had fought against Bavuraat, struggling desperately to keep his supper down without having to spring to his feet and rush from among them.

Zaide chuckled. 'You have mentioned it again. We will not do so, nor will we eat meat in front of you. This thing of tolerance and consideration – it must be mutual. Yes, my post is hereditary. It would have fallen to my son, and thence to Zaire. My son is dead. When I die, Zaire will be Keeper. It is a lonely life. I do not rule in Oridorna – no one does, as there are rulers among the Orisans and those Outside. Insofar as we have authority over others, the son of the Keeper is leader, and the Keeper is . . .'

'Outside,' Cleve said, 'I think you might be called priest.'

'Perhaps. You must be careful with the sidsorn Zaire has given you, Cleve. It is deadly to you as to the man at whom you point it. Never take off its top. Never hold it so that the flapdoor faces you. To use it, one merely hooks one's thumb in the loop of gut, and draws it down. The flapdoor at the other end of the box opens. The emanation is released.

'I assumed as much,' Cleve said, although I did not try it – I thought it wise to wait for instruction. What is inside?'

Zaide shrugged. 'Is that correct?'

'I – sir? What?'

'The shrug.' Zaide raised his thin old shoulders again. He was very thin, with the round little belly, however, of an old man.

Cleve smiled. 'Oh. Yes. Thank you.'

'I must teach the children. Inside the box, Cleve, is some of the rockfire. Those who dig it from the mountain die. We have not many of them, and we make another only when one ceases to function. There is a smooth surface inside, too, that directs the ray – Jaire, bring us one of the empty alsidorn.'

She left them to return with one of the little stone deathboxes. She handed it to her grandfather.

'It is safe to open,' Zaide said, handing it to Cleve.

Cleve accepted and opened it, not without some trepidation. 'A smooth surface inside,' Zaide had told him, 'to direct the ray.' Yes. It was a mirror, of some polished stone like basalt or obsidian. It was deep blue, and as Cleve turned it he saw several other shades of blue in its strange depths. There was a space, too, for the rocklight, a small, toothed depression. The teeth would hold it there, glowing safely, as he knew the one in the pouch was glowing, even now. When the opening in the end of the box was tripped, the full force of whatever ray – gamma? – the stuff emitted was bounced from the three mirrorlike surfaces, thus channeled out the awful little 'doorway' of the deathbox. To kill.

The strip of llico hide that tripped the door – the trigger, Cleve mused. The little door, neatly fitted into a groove on either side so that it swung easily when the cord was pulled, swung shut immediately the pressure was released – the barrel. The mirror surfaces could be called the firing pin; apparently they made the ray deadly, by concentrating and aiming it. And the rocklight – the ammunition.

It was without doubt the crudest, simplest – and most deadly – gun ever created by imaginative, resourceful man. And it was that – a gun. A ray-gun, on a planet just at the level of smelting iron into steel swords and too-heavy armor! And evolved, not by some ultracivilized nation of warriors, but by a Stone Age people who used the terrible little weapon only in defense. With it, with a few of them, Andor could be conquered, all Andor. By people with sight; their inability to distinguish between inanimate objects, whether sentient or no, was the Oridorns' fatal disadvantage. It would make them easy prey for anyone with the sense to remain still, were the Oridorns in the open where they could be attacked in any sort of mass.

'How is it the Orisans never acquired any of these?' Cleve asked, thinking of the obvious.

'They know we have them. We never carry one below. Today one went down for the first time – it was an emergency. You are a friend of Oridorna, and had rescued two of our own and remained behind to fight off their pursuers. We had to aid you. We know of but four connections to Orisana. To our knowledge they have never tried to clamber up the way you came, but it, like the other three shafts, is perpetually guarded by us. When we descend, we take only swords and daggers. We know how vulnerable we are, Cleve, and we know we must never allow the Orisans or the Orimors to have one of these weapons. We also – we also fear, and assume, that someday it will happen. Someday, somehow, it will happen. And they will use it to destroy us, getting more and more to use against us until Oridorn is no more. And then perhaps they will try to make their own.'

'Who manufactures them?'

'The Keeper. I have made none. My father made one; it

was to replace one that had ceased to function. We do not know why it happens, nor do we have any idea in advance that it will happen.'

'Giving me one – does that mean it must be replaced?'

'Yes.'

'But – you said that he who brings the rocklight from the mountain dies.'

'Yes.'

'Then I cannot take this!'

'You must accept it. It is our gift. I have already begun work on another only a few sleeps ago. It is as simple to make two. The boxes are ready, now. You hold one of them.'

Cleve looked about at their impassive faces, flickeringly visible in the light of his single torch. 'But – that will cost two lives?'

'Oh, no,' Zaide told him. 'Only one. The work must be done swiftly, and two may be made at the cost of but one life. It is well spent, you see. It is for Oridorna.'

'You were going to make one anyhow?'

'Yes, Cleve. You see, I am dying. I know it, Zaire knows it; he is soon to be Keeper. And we have told Jaire. I will die, and be greatly honored by my people, and – but we will not speak of that before you.'

And your grandchildren and sister will eat you, Cleve thought. He said, 'What does your death have to do with it, Zaide?'

'But everything! As I said, I am dying anyhow. I *know* it, and we will not discuss how or why. I am old, and I am dying. I decided that I would die as Keeper, and make two of the deathboxes before I go. That way, perhaps Zaire will never have to make one.'

'Oh.' Cleve gazed at the old man, whom he now realized was one of the bravest, noblest men he'd ever met. 'Only the Keeper makes the deathbox. And he who brings the rocklight from the mountain dies. And – that is the Keeper's duty.'

The old man nodded, obviously proud of the ability. 'Of course.'

Chapter Sixteen

The Eyes of Oridorna

Cleve learned that only the deaf and those with otherwise impaired hearing were 'blind' among the Oridorns. A few questions gave him most of the answer to their eyeless sight.

It was sonar; echolocation. It was an active process in which the Oridorns emitted sounds of extremely high frequency, far past the upper limits of human hearing – 20,000 cycles per second. With their highly sophisticated biological sonar, they navigated, simply by generating a sound, then identifying objects and obstacles and their approximate distance by their reflected echoes. Banished forever to live out their lives without light, they lost the reason for possessing eyes, then the eyes themselves. And at some time, probably simultaneously, they developed the echolocative process.

Nearby objects they 'saw' in terms of the physical parameters of their own UHF cries, returning to them from those objects. By the same process they were able to perceive size and shape and mobility of the object. A rock or a man standing against a wall could be discerned almost instantly; not until it moved would the Oridorn know by echolocative sense whether it was animate or otherwise. Cleve had no means of measuring. Knowing something of *Eptesicus fuscus*, the big, insectivorous brown bat of Earth, Cleve assumed the sounds emitted by Jaire and her people were in the 50,000-cycles-per-second area. They could readily distinguish the shape of objects, although this power was diminished by distance. Given two objects at varying distances from themselves, they established quickly which was the closer – merely by noting the difference in arrival time of the echoes from the two objects.

Fascinated, he experimented, although he was aware that his simple tests were far from acceptable by Earthside standards, far from what are called 'controlled experiments.'

Given a rock shaped somewhat like a man and of similar height and width, Jaire could distinguish it as rock, not man, only when she was within about fifteen feet of it.

Herein lay their danger. A man might stand absolutely motionless and allow himself to be approached quite closely by an Oridorn. Worse, if Cleve stood among rock outcroppings, Jaire was hard put to say which was he and which the boulders or stalagmites – and even then, *knowing* he was there.

God creates, he mused, *and God compensates. Or Mama Nature, or Daron, or Prime Mover, or whatever source you choose for attribution of natural phenomena – no matter how unnatural.*

The water of these strange people came from the same source as that of the Orisans: slender mountain streams. The Oridorns had wood for torches, which they had taken from slain Orisans. Cleve carefully waited until his slow-burning glim was nearly out, then lighted another from it. True, the deady little 'gun' in his pouch could serve him as a flashlight, of sorts; it emitted a barely visible beam. He felt sure the rocklight in the Cavern of Death in Oridorna must be different from that illuminating Orisana – it was not nearly so luminous, and surely it was far more dangerous. They showed him that its ray would not pass through rock, not even the thinnest shalelike slab. Then they demonstrated what it did to mushroom and bone and llico hide: It blackened and holed them, almost instantly. Since he had decided to keep the deathbox with him, to try by its use to ensure his passage through the Orimors above; he did not want to weaken it by using it for illumination.

On the other hand, he knew that if his torch went out, he would be helpless in the labyrinthine 'city' of Oridorna. The darkness was absolute. Only one who had been in a cave deep underground, without artificial light and with not the tiniest aperture for the admission of outside light, could appreciate the existence of total darkness, an impenetrable black deeper than the cloudiest moonless midnight, the most tightly shuttered room.

Cleve lay again on a bed formed by laying the white pelts

over the bare stone of the cavern floor. Jaire and several other women were at work, making a whitefurred suit for his projected departure from their caverns into the undoubted slashing cold of the mountaintop. In Oridorna as in Orisana, the dark caverns were not cold. He had no explanation. It was not that the air and the rock were warm; it was just that they were not cold, as might have beeen expected. Perhaps, he thought, it was another property of the rocklight. Or perhaps there was another element within this great, honeycombed mountain that provided warmth. Even the water from the little underground streams was barely cool, warmed as it trickled down from the snow atop the mountain.

Doralan Andrah. Doralan Andrah. Doralan Andrah of—

—of Andor.

He could not remember. He realized now that this was not natural; certainly Gordon on Earth had told him more about Doralan Andrah than he now knew. Certainly the bespectacled, brown-suited man had told him the name of Andrah's city, and even surrounding lands. It was not just that he had not been inbued, as promised, with Andrah's memory. Cleve now knew. Nor was it simply a matter of his having forgotten what he had known.

It was not just the absence of a positive, his condition. It was a negative.

Knowledge had been stolen from his mind. Somehow, he had been robbed of what Andorite knowledge he possessed. If that were so, then—

Cleve sat suddenly erect in the darkness.

If that were so, then perhaps Gordon's organization *had* provided him with memories of Doralan Andrah! Perhaps they, too, had been stolen; all had been stripped from his mind save what he remembered *as Robert Cleve.* The language and customs – these had been hynotically implanted in his brain; he had *learned* them, mnemonically, if mechanistically. The memories of Andrah – those he had *acquired*, without actually learning: Gordon had explained to him that all Doralan knew would be imprinted on his mind as information was imprinted in the 'mind' of a computer.

Cleve pursued the thought, worrying it, tugging it, striving to conduct unexpected raids on secret corners of his mind. He could not lead himself, could not trick himself, could not trap himself into remembering. He knew no names, either of persons or of places, save Doralan Andrah. He knew Doralan Andrah possessed power and position; he could not remember over whom or what. He knew Doralan Andrah had an important mission and was dying, and Cleve was to take over his body – as he had – and perform that mission. As he had not. He could not even remember what the mission was.

And with that he dragged, by its slender and tenuous tail, another idea into his roiling brain.

Perhaps – perhaps he had been here longer than he knew? Perhaps it was *on Andor* that he had lost his memory! Naturally, somehow, or . . . unnaturally. Via hypnotism, perhaps.

Or . . . sorcery?

Well, once hypnotism had been thought sorcerous, arcane, on Earth. There were still many who feared it with the same superstitious awe that prevented their walking beneath ladders or entering cemeteries at midnight. It was science; a method of making direct contact with the superpowerful subconscious mind. Its applications in medicine; in espionage, in police work, were enormous.

Perhaps . . . here . . . sorcery was . . . science?

He did not like that thought. True, his head was full of Andoran words having to do with magic, respectful words without any hint of semihumorous or disbelieving connotations. It would have to be proved to him. He could not accept sorcery.

'Perhaps,' he muttered into the subterranean darkness of Oridorna, 'perhaps it has been!'

He jerked his head at the gasp his voice elicited. 'Who's there?'

'Cleve – it is Jaire.'

'Jaire, you must not come silently upon me again. You walk in barefoot silence, and you have three times now shocked me, caused my heart to leap, and cost me several gray hairs by stealing upon me.'

'I am sorry,' she said softly. 'What – what is gray hairs?'

He chuckled. 'A sign of age,' he told her, 'among my people. Like wrinkled skin,' he added, realizing she would know about that; these people were fascinated by textures. Indeed, among them the wrinkled, the skinny – whose skin was thus not smooth and taut – were considered beautiful. Their flesh offered more to the Oridorn sense of touch. In Oridorna, the old had at last come to be considered as beautiful! No woman here disguised her wrinkles.

'Did you say something else?' Jaire asked. She was a barely visible column of ghostly gray-white in his chamber; he had propped the torch in a corner to provide as little light as possible. There were no sconces in Oridorna. 'As I came in, I mean.'

'Uh – oh, no, I was muttering to myself, if I must admit it. I spoke to you after I heard you gasp. Don't creep up on me anymore. Say something. Make a noise. Hm – I just realized. Your people, if awake, would know you were coming?'

'Of course, without trying. I am sorry, Cleve. I will make a noise. She clapped her hands. 'Will that do?'

'Admirably. Perhaps a little less exuberantly.' He started to ask her why she'd come, then instead asked, 'Jaire . . . what do you know of sorcery?'

'Sorcery? Nothing. Very little. We have understood that it is practiced Outside, by women. It is called Starpower. They are the Starpowered Ones.'

That set off no alarums in Cleve's brain, prompted no memories. He possessed the words; he possessed what was probably the only complete Andoran vocabulary on Andor.

'They are . . . real? I mean, they can really ensorcel?'

'So we understand. There are no Starpowered Ones among us, or among the Orisans, although the Treemen slaves say some of their women have the power. They believe it, I know that.'

'Um. What – what can these Starpowered Ones do?'

Her answer was simple and succinct: 'Anything, I think.'

'Anything! Doesn't that astonish you? Frighten you?'

'It does not concern me. Perhaps I am Starpowered. But I would not know how to exercise the power. Perhaps one must have eyes, or perhaps one must have what you call "color." No, I do not think about it. There are many things Outside, we know, that we do not understand.'

He sighed. Well, he'd ask again – Outside. 'Why are you here, Jaire?'

'I have told my brother and my grandfather and my aunt,' she said. 'My brother and my grandfather have touched you, and they understand. You are warm, and you rescued me. I owe you my life, even though you freed me of the debt. But I came here to beg of you your warmth.'

Her use of the word 'beg' made it more difficult. Had she said 'I want you to share your warmth with me' or 'I want your warmth' or some such, it would have been easier to tell the eyeless woman to . . . get lost. The fact that another *wanted* or *asked* for or even *needed* something had never given Cleve a feeling of obligation or guilt; what he had had on Earth, what little he had here, he had got by his own efforts. In this situation, though . . .

'Jaire, you remember what happened before. Another wanted my warmth, and liked it to the point of being perfectly willing to maim me to keep it with her, or to slay me to prevent my taking it elsewhere.' *My warmth*, he thought, in a mental snort.

'I know,' her little voice said.

He would have preferred to look elsewhere, but found he could not. In the semidarkness she was lovely and feminine; a nude blonde standing a few feet away. He could not see, in the unsteady light of the flickering brand, her strange, veined skin, her near-transparent hair, her weirdly eyeless face. He could see only that she was a pale, shapely young female interestingly half-lit by the frenetic ebb and flow of torchlight. A breakable young female, very possibly.

And he was a man.

'I know,' she said again. 'But I am not Siraa. She would enslave you – she will enslave Shilaat if he takes her to mate. I assure you. I would be your slave.' Jaire came a few paces forward and went to her knees beside his pallet, her arms a little apart from her body, her hands open – as, probably, she had been taught befit a slave in Orisana during her captivity there. Her unclothed breasts were trembling ivory in the fitful, pale illumination from his glim. 'I am your slave, Cleve. Accept me as your slave.'

'Don't be silly, Jaire,' he said, deliberately using words to cut. 'You are the granddaughter of the Keeper, the sister of the leader. I am an Outsider, and I am leaving for the Outside – immediately.'

'When it is time to wake?'

'Perhaps,' he said, thinking of the timelessness for dwellers in perpetual darkness. There was no morning in Oridorna, no moon, no night. There was a time to wake, a time to sleep, and times to eat. And no clocks, no sun, no stars. Only life and death marked the passage of time here, among these people. They had one shorter measurement, of course: the women.

'Well, then, if you leave when it is time to wake, I will be your slave until then.'

'Jaire—'

'I have told you: My brother and my grandfather understand. I have told them. I am not a maiden – Shilaat was brutal in that. I beg you for warmth. I beg you for one experience I shall remember all my life. I beg you to accept me as your slave, Cleve.'

'You are my slave, Jaire. Come share my warmth.'

A hood of soft hide covered with long, silken white hair shielded his head and most of his face. He wore a tunic of the same white fur over leggings of the same stuff, and they had fashioned boots for him, the women of Oridorna. Over the snowsuit thus formed, Cleve slung two thin baldrics, preventing them from shifting overmuch with his movements by a third strip of llico, around his waist. On his left hip was the curved sword he had taken from Bavuraat; spoils of combat. On his right swung the little pouch containing the Oridorn deathbox. His long-furred mittens were stuck in what served him as a belt.

At the foot of a long tunnel sloping gently upward from

Oridorna, Cleve bade farewell to the gentle people of this impossible land. Two warriors would accompany him; he had persuaded the old man Zaide and his grandson Zaire and granddaughter Jaire to take their leave of him here.

'I am indebted and grateful to all of you,' Robert Cleve said, looking at their forever-impassive faces.

All their faces, he had noticed, looked sad. Perhaps it was the lack of eyes, perhaps it was that they had never seen facial expressions. Perhaps it was that they were indeed sad. Without eyes, without lachrymal glands, they were denied the release of tears, even as infants. Perhaps they would always be sad, doomed from birth to possess no outlet for their fears, their pains, their anguish. They could not weep.

'You have shown us that other people are not necessarily enemies, Cleve of Earth,' old Zaide said. 'You are the first guest within the collective memory of Oridorna. You are the first man not of Oridorna to be called Warrior of Oridorna. You have provided us with knowledge, and history. You will be long remembered and spoken of among us.'

'Until death,' Jaire said in her soft, sad voice, and Cleve felt a tightening in his throat, the growing of a lump. The woman, he knew, would present a tear-streaming face were she able. What, he wondered, was their release? Or had they any?

He touched them one by one, Zaire gripping his hand and touching its palm as he had that other time, in the cavern of Orisana. No weapons: friends.

'Nor will I ever forget Oridorna and my friends here,' Cleve said, and felt proof of his own possession of tear ducts. Despite the fact that there was none to see, he turned. 'Let's go.'

He and his two guides, both armed with the Oridorn deathboxes, made their way up into darkness. Cleve carried the torch he alone needed.

'The way may be clear,' the man with the belly said, 'or they may be there – the Orimors.'

'Certainly they will be close by,' the other man, the muscular one, said.

Cleve nodded and plodded on, ever upward. The darkness

spun away as they advanced; intimidated by his torch. It closed in behind them again, as if following them like some dangerous beast just without the radius of his brand's illumination.

They rounded several turns, passed through a particularly tight squeeze between smoothed, outjutting granite, and ascended. There was a little dip, then a climb over the fallen rubble of a long-ago rockfall from the stony ceiling, then a steeper climb.

'Here,' the muscular Oridorn said, halting and putting out a hand. They had been walking along beside a narrow little serpent of trickling water for many, many paces. The stream, when Cleve tested it, grew steadily colder as they ascended beside it.

'There is a curve in the passage ahead, Cleve. Just beyond that is the opening onto the mountain. Can you hear the wind?'

Cleve admitted he could not, and the man sighed; how pitiful were all but those of Oridorna! With their weakened hearing, they could depend only upon the things they called 'eyes' – which were of no value whatever when they were without what they called 'light!'

'A moment, then,' Cleve said. 'I will put out the torch by dipping it in the water. You can pick it up as you return.'

He did, laying the torch across the path. 'Be careful not to stumble over it in the da—' he began, and stopped himself. The stomachy Oridorn chuckled. They now stood in darkness – but it was no longer absolute. Somewhere ahead, there was light. The three men stood in a gray world, and Cleve stared about him.

How long it had been! Even this dim, filtered daylight, seeping in through the opening ahead and creeping around a bend in the tunnelway, was beautiful to a man so long denied the sight of sun and moon – moons – and stars.

They went forward and rounded the tunnel bend.

And there was the world of light.

Cleve squinted.

After perhaps a minute of squinting, letting his pupils grow accustomed to the light, letting his eyes accustom themselves, glut themselves on the ruddy sky of Andor, seen through the low natural doorway ahead, he turned to his companions. They were shivering.

'Go back,' he said. 'What can you do to help me from here? I will crawl out, keeping as low as possible. Me they might take for one of themselves, at least temporarily. You they'd attack at once.'

'We will wait here,' the muscular guide said.

Cleve closed a cold hand on the man's icy arm. 'Thank you. I am going now. Go back.'

And he went alone up the passage, toward a ruddy sky grayed by wind-swirled snow, toward a moaning, howling wind, toward inimical beast-men and inimical elements and – the unknown.

Chapter Seventeen

The Beast-Men of Orimora

The mountaintop was a ragged white vista falling away below him on both sides. It was not the mountaintop, strictly speaking; the peak rose up behind him, a challenge of snow-covered rock. An angry wind thrust at him, pulled at him, attempting to hurl him from his place where he had no business being. This was the domain of wind and snow and ice and chill sunlight. The wind howled as it attacked him, howled and moaned like ghost-voices inviting a newcomer to their icy ranks. The snow glittered; it was cold snow, ski snow, and he knew the temperature here was closer to zero Fahrenheit than to freezing.

The opening to the cavern whencc he'd come was no more than four feet high, and he had crawled forth, his furry mittens protecting his already cold hands. The wind stung his eyes so that they were immediately blurred with tears. He pulled lower his furry hood, drawing it up, too, over his mouth and nose so that only his slitted eyes were forced to take the wind's icy assault.

He saw nothing, no one. When he rolled onto his back to gaze upward at the peak, there was nothing there save an unwelcoming Nature. Vision was limited; the wind swirled snow that filled the air and clouded it, bringing the tears to his eyes. He wiped them away and waited before moving until they came no more. He looked down.

The snow-covered mountain vanished into the snow-filled air – and into clouds and mist, wispy shapes that wreathed the mountain and nudged it cautiously, as if to test its cold bite.

He began to crawl downward. Another pause; another reconnoiter. Still he saw no signs of life.

Cleve rose to stand tall and challenging on the mountainside. He turned slowly, looking about him on the three sides left open to his vision. Nothing. Only the snow, mounded and jagged as it clung to the mountain's rough face. And behind him – a steady, empty slope to the top.

He was helpless not to do what he did. It had been in his race since time began, infecting the race of Man like a non-malignant cancer that, many times, had proved very malignant indeed.

He made his way up to the very peak and there left one of the strips of dried fish the Oridorns had pressed upon him. Into its hard surface, already freezing though dry, he scratched his name. And when he had finished, he smiled a wry smile and added another name.

Robert Cleve. And Doralan Andrah.

Then he turned and began to descend – toward the clouds.

He had descended some forty feet – ten of which he slid, without injury or more than minor pain – when they appeared.

They rose up around him, ghost-shapes in the gray air of their domain. The Orimors.

They were tall; he had known that, from their hides. Closer to seven feet than six, and some, he judged, were taller than that. They were shaggy and white, as of course he had known they would be, with their beautiful pelts of snowy silk, many of the individual hairs being as many as three inches long. Their hands must have been tough, he thought at that first sight. Their backs were as furry as their bodies, but the palms were devoid of it, dark and leathery-looking. They were four-fingered, as he was, with an apposable thumb. Hairy or not, savage or not, they were close to being men.

Their eyes were nearly invisible in their hairy faces, and he saw that there was yellow within those narrow sight slits. A bit of unfurred forehead showed, the fur growing down to a long widow's peak on each, ending just above the bushy, craggy brows. He assumed they had ears; they were fur-buried. Their noses were small and flat, the same grayish-black as their palms. They stood very erect, far more like men than Earthly gorillas or chimpanzees.

'The Abominable Snowmen,' he muttered. 'Perhaps some

of them have got to Earth? Or perhaps some from Earth have somehow come here, to Andor. Certainly these are the creatures we know are in Tibet and Wisconsin!'

They wore only their fur and arms. Baldrics and belts, swords and daggers, spears. None carried shields. There was no possibility of their accepting him, even in this whirling snow, as one of themselves. They were taller, far broader. And of course their faces were not his face, and the mittens he wore only superficially resembled their hands.

Very slowly he let his right mitten slip off, wiping it off against his own white-haired thigh. Very slowly he doubled those instantly cold fingers, squeezing hard, then plucked at his little pouch with them.

One of the Orimors launched a spear. A spear is not like an arrow or a bullet; there is plenty of time for the target to duck, if he sees the cast. Even at twenty feet, Cleve jerked aside from the shaft that swished toward him – and shot past, several feet of wood shod with metal.

He raised his left hand, palm toward them. He spoke, loudly, the Andorite word for peace.

One of the Orimors shrieked at him, the sound not unlike that emitted by an Earthly panther or mountain lion. He waved his sword and started forward. Another drew back his spear, sighted, and launched it.

Cleve whipped up the Oridorn deathbox and got his thumb into the cord loop and pulled. He swung his hand as he lunged aside from the onrushing spear.

The spear's haft, curving slightly in its flight, actually touched his hide-covered side. He heard the hissing sound as it kicked up snow behind him. At the same time he watched the effect of his defense.

The pelt of the spear thrower blackened at the chest. The creature sank without a cry. The yeti-like creature beside him looked down in horror at the blackening area of his own pelt, on his left hip, and bellowed in pain. He lunged forward, taking three long steps before he, too, collapsed.

Cleve didn't want to kill all of them. He wondered – briefly – if he had a choice. They ringed him on three sides; a quick glance showed him none above him. He did not want to go upward again, and right now his back was a target. His glance showed him a cluster of snow-covered rocks a few feet downmountain, and he dived for the partial cover they offered.

An iceball whizzed past his head. He had moved just in time; one of the snowmen behind him had launched a natural missile. Of course. There was no vegetation up here; nothing from which to make spears. The spears, like their scimitars, came from the men living at the base of the mountain. Natural weapons could be quickly created here on the cold mountainside. Snowballs, squeezed until they were dry. For that matter, a dagger of ice could be fashioned pretty swiftly. If it were used just as swiftly, it would be as effective as stone or perhaps steel.

His enemies set up a shout – animal screams – as he leaped. He plunged among the five or six tall rocks clustered there, covered with snow so that they formed a sort of white sanctuary. He struck the ground among them – and it opened and swallowed him.

Cleve crashed down onto a hard surface but a few feet below. Snow tumbled after him as he struck and rolled, floundering. He had lost his left mitten, now, and his hand contacted something soft and silky. A pelt? Yes – a pelt on its original owner. It moved.

Cleve rolled onto his back and looked up to see the scimitar rushing down at him in the manlike hand of its Orimor wielder. Cleve did not bother with his weapons; he rolled aside as fast as he could move.

The sword struck the rock where he'd lain with a loud clang as Cleve scrambled onto his side. He still clutched the Oridorn 'gun'; he swung it up and triggered it. He watched his attacker go staggering back, dying soundlessly. He – or it – collapsed against the stone wall a few feet away and sank slowly down to die sitting up with its chin on its chest.

I'd be dead, Cleve thought, *without this weapon! I'd never have got even this far; they'd have killed me up there, from a distance. My sword was as useless up there as a club. Worse, I could have thrown the club with something approaching accuracy!*

'Daron preserve!' a voice cried, and Cleve looked quickly in its direction.

The man rose slowly, shivering; he wore dark furs, but his head and hands were unclothed, and his parka-like garment was open at the throat.

'Daron preserve and bless! *A man!*'

'Get that sword,' Cleve said. 'We're far from out of this. There are—'

No need to tell the man of the Orimors above. One dropped into the little room, formed by a shallow pocket in the mountainside hardly meriting the name 'crevasse.' The creature alit on its furry, padded-soled feet, and it emitted an Orimor shriek as it landed, crouching. Its sword swung up. And Cleve shot it with the strange Oridorn ray-gun.

It collapsed across the body of its fellow, the sword clanging. The other man snatched it up. His big eyes went from Cleve to the opening above; their vault was perhaps ten feet deep and seven or eight feet on a side, slightly wedge-shaped. Cleve looked up.

The iceball, fortunately, went low and struck him in the right shoulder. Even through the furry clothing he wore, the impact of that hard-packed missile from a distance of no more than eleven or twelve feet was heavy and painful. His arm jerked. His fingers opened spasmodically. The deathbox slipped from his grip; he heard the little click of rock on rock as the counterbalanced 'door' swung shut.

The Orimor who had flung the icy missile sprang up from where it crouched on the lip of the pit. It leaped down on Cleve.

He had no time to roll from its way. That tall, heavy body struck him full force, and he gasped and fought desperately for breath even while his hands leaped out to grasp his attacker. Its hands, too, came for him – arching for his throat. Cleve tore ineffectually at its furry pelt as those powerful fingers, three of them fully six inches long, closed like iron bands about his neck. Cleve grabbed the shaggy arms and exerted all his strength in an effort to push them away.

He might as well have sought to change the direction of

the wind blowing across the mountain. His head began to feel swollen, hot, and he knew he was being strangled.

The Orimor's mouth opened wide, revealing teeth more animal than manlike, with long, yellowish canines. From that red-tongued maw came a gargling scream. Almost at once blood bubbled forth. The fingers loosened about Cleve's throat; sucking in a great breath, he shook his roaring head, and hurled the hairy arms away. He scrambled from beneath the body as the other man withdrew his bloody sword from its back.

For a moment they looked at each other, two men without names or countries, who had met suddenly and violently on a mountainside. They might be enemies or brothers; at another time and another place they might have passed each other without a word – or they might have fought. Here they were allies: Both were black-haired, copper-skinned men, and the Orimors were a deadly, inhuman enemy that united them.

'There are more?'

Cleve nodded, picked up the deathbox with his left hand while he held his right fist close to his mouth and huffed warm breath on it. 'There are more.'

They stood there, waiting in panting silence, staring up at the square opening to the sky.

'Cleve! Cleve!' The voices were tenuous riders on the howling wind.

'Here!' Cleve shouted.

'We have slain them all!' The shout came back, faintly.

'Then get back inside before you freeze,' Cleve bellowed. 'I'll make it down; I have found another Outsider!'

He turned a grinning face on the other man, who was staring at him with a puzzled frown. Cleve's mind raced; he did not want to begin their camaraderie by lying, but he did not want, either, to tell this man or any other about the Oridorns.

'Friends,' he said, and waved the deadly little box he held. 'They have these. We are free to get out of here.'

'Sorcery,' the other shrugged. 'But – how do we get out?'

Cleve looked around. 'I am afraid we are going to have to

use the bodies of our late enemies,' he said. 'How long will it take them to freeze?'

They climbed out, Cleve and Barke of Sharne, on the semifrozen corpses of the two Orimors they had slain. Bracing themselves against the wind, they looked about.

There were no corpses. Cleve's guides must have heard the Orimor roars and screams and come running to help their friend, despite the cold that must affect their pale, cool bodies far worse and far more quickly than those of normal men. Perhaps they had seen his plunge; perhaps not. They had slain the remaining members of the Orimor band that had attacked him, then called his name until he answered, indicating he was unhurt.

Then, while he and Barke had waited, stamping their feet and slapping their arms and exchanging names, for the cold to stiffen the bodies of the Orimors they had slain, the men of Oridorna had collected the corpses of their own kill. They had taken, also, the two Cleve had slain on the mountainside with the Oridorn sidsorn.

He did not even shudder. Man or beast, the Orimors were not such gentle, friendly people as the Oridorns. And the Oridorns needed meat.

He hoped Jaire would make something pretty for herself from one of the pelts; a snowy little loincloth, perhaps, such as the one that had so fetchingly decorated the hips of Siraa of Orisana.

The other man looked around. 'They are gone,' he said. 'The other Orimors, and your friends.' He looked questioningly at Cleve.

Cleve nodded. 'Pai,' he said.

'You are certain there were others?'

'I killed two of them,' Cleve said. 'You can see the splotch of blood over there, on the snow.'

'And now all are gone,' Barke gazed at him. 'Sorcery,' he said, without sarcasm or shudder. Andor was not Earth! 'Are you going to vanish now, too?'

'I wish I could,' Cleve grinned, shaking his head. 'No, I have my sidsorn, but I must climb and slide down the mountain, just like you. We'd better get started; your face isn't protected.'

'I am more than ready,' Barke said. 'I wish you could vanish – and take me with you. What is a sidsorn?'

Cleve held up the deathbox, the Andorite ray-gun.

'Ah. The sorcerous thing that slew that Orimor – I've never seen death hurled so quietly and so swiftly. And so fierily – it burned his pelt!'

'It is deadly. Please, please don't touch it. It—' Cleve was going to say 'is complicated,' when his new friend interrupted.

'I assure you,' Barke said with feeling, 'I won't touch it! I've no touch for sorcery – and I've never met a Starpowered *man* before. Well met, Cleve of Earth. I am glad we met as friends; you would not make a pleasant enemy. Where is Earth?'

Cleve shook his head. 'Far away,' he said. 'I cannot even tell you its direction.' Which was true; all Cleve knew was that Earth was somewhere up there, in the Andorite sky. He had even less idea where lay his Andorite home – or rather that of Doralan Andrah. Which reminded him: 'Do you know the name Doralan Andrah?'

'No. Should I?'

'I suppose not.' They were moving downward, carefully, several feet apart. 'Where is Sharne?'

Barke nodded: 'Below those clouds. Once we've climbed below them, we will see it, and the ocean. You don't know Sharne?'

'No. Should I?'

Barke laughed. 'Of course,' he said. 'But – you must not go there with me. We must part, Cleve, once we're down below the snows and can see – for many miles. Many miles,' he added, dreamily.

'Part? Why? Perhaps in Sharne I can find a way to get home. Surely I can find some clothes and something to eat.'

'No, Cleve,' Barke said quietly, and his words barely came to Cleve's ears; they'd have been lost had Barke not been upwind of him. 'You must not go with me to Sharne. There is only one kind of stranger, only one kind of visitor, to mighty Sharne.'

'Yes?' Cleve slid down several feet, reaching for the hand Barke extended. Barke gripped it in his own icy fingers, and his dark eyes drilled sadly into Cleve's.

'Yes,' Barke of Sharne said. 'The only kind of newcomer to Sharne is – a slave.'

PART THREE
Doralan Andrah

Chapter Eighteen

The Freedman of Sharne

They sat together on the mountainside, in the warming rays of Andor's red-orange sun. They had been careful, clapping their hands and thrusting them within their furry garments to warm them beneath their arms. Neither of them was certain that his fingers were not frostbitten, or that those stiff little lumps at the ends of his feet were not going to come off with the boots.

They had struggled and slid and fallen and rolled and cursed and stumbled their way down the mountainside. They had entered the clouds and gasped and struggled on, ever downward, until they emerged dripping. Dripping; the clouds were not ice-laden, not snow-laden. They were just clouds, and temperature mist. The temperature had risen steadily as they made their way downward. Below the clouds it must have leaped upward another ten degrees.

Cleve thrust back his white-furred hood and laughed and went on; the slope was dotted with outjutting rocks and monster boulders that had rolled and slid down long ago, and were now anchored in place, baubles decorating the mountain's lower, gentle slopes.

Now they sat on a flat shelf of rock, warmed by the sun that bathed it most of each day. Slowly, gradually, piece by piece, they loosened and then stripped off the heavy clothing they no longer needed.

Directly below was Sharne.

It began at the mountain's foot – indeed, some homes, those of the wealthy, dotted the first slopes. The city then sprawled out across the plain to the banks of the ocean. It stretched out, a purplish, barely ruffled surface, to join hands with the horizon: the Placid Sea. The dock was full of ships; sailing craft with a single square sail and a small, forward-leaning sail that thrust out over the bow. And there were galleys, with one and two banks of oars, low-slung vessels whose midsections seemed to kiss the water lapping just below their gunwales.

Sharne was bright, a city built of colored stone and stucco and painted brightly, like a great scintillant jewel left on the shore by some long-ago giant who'd removed it before wading out into the sea. Most of the buildings were low; Cleve assumed some stiff winds came in from the ocean now and then, and a towered city would be endangered.

Barke of Sharne quickly corroborated that; many towers had been constructed, in the old days, and had been destroyed with tremendous loss of life within and beneath when they crashed down to shatter the buildings at their feet. Now a law prohibited buildings above two storeys or a certain height. That sprawling, Y-shaped collection of snowy white was the royal palace of Sharnan Vreen, Andorgrof.

'Andorgrof!' Cleve echoed, turning wide eyes to his new friend.

Barke nodded. 'Andorgrof,' he repeated. 'Ruler of the world. And so he believes. And so they believe, most of them. It is the mightiest city in the world, Sharne. The mightiest navy. It trades far far asea. Sharnese ships have gone farther than any other. We touch many ports whose ships have never durst come here.'

'So *they* believe, you said. But yourself?'

'I know that Sharne is the mightiest city in the world, yes,' Barke said. 'But no one rules the world. Sharnan Vreen is Grof of Sharne, nothing more, and that is entirely enough! Surely Sharne is also the world's wealthiest land.'

'I can believe that,' Cleve said. He had no basis for comparison, after all. He had never seen another Andorite city – that he could recall. He wondered what Barke would say if he were told he was the first truly human human Cleve had ever seen – that he could recall. 'But – if they believe it, Barke, why don't you?'

'I am not Sharnese. Not by birth, I mean. I am a citizen, now, and a freedman. I am mate on a ship . . . I do not see it in harbor. But I came here as a slave. Do you know of Eth?'

Cleve shook his head.

'It is far to the north; I am not even certain where it lies. It is a land but recently up from what some call barbarism. Many of us were unable to accept the new life. There are probably more men of Eth scattered across the world than from anyplace else. They are mercenaries, lovers of fighting. Sixty-eight years ago Eth conquered its neighbor to the south, Valnyra. Valnyra is a farming land, a country of arbors and superb wine. Eth did not hold it long. The Ethites were driven back, mainly by the clansmen from Elgain, which lies south of Valnyra. Eth signed a treaty with both nations, but that did not mean the men of Eth settled down to become farmers. You will find them all over the world, as mercenaries.'

'Is that how you came to Sharne?'

'Not exactly.' Barke gazed down at the brightly colored city below. 'When my father left Eth, my mother insisted on accompanying him. I was born in some country whose name I forget – we moved on. In Jamuga, my father sold his services to the king and fought against the Syrhanese. When that war ended, he still could not settle; he took employment in the Syrhanese marines. He sailed on their merchant ships, with a band of other warriors, to defend the ships if need be. On his last voyage I joined him. I was thirteen. We were struck by a storm at sea, and the ship and most hands went down. My father died, but he is back on Andor, I know. After such a life he was not granted a warrior's death! His crimes in previous lives must have been fearsome, for Daron to have denied him eternal retirement.'

'Perhaps in this life he is less a wanderer,' Cleve said, 'and happier. And perhaps he will have the opportunity to die a warrior's death and thus join Daron's legion of heroes in the Final Life.'

'It is good to think so,' Barke said. 'Thank you – but he was happy, as I was, and my mother. At any rate, some eleven of us survived. We drifted for days, and were barely alive when a Sharnese merchantman picked us up. That is how I learned that one comes to Sharne only as a slave. The Sharnese believe that they are superior to everyone else in the world. I went again to sea – as a slave. I made six voyages as such, until I saved my captain's life one day. I am not sure why. He had a man whipped, and a few days later I looked up to see the man stealing up behind the captain with a dagger. I shouted and sprang on him. I was freed that day, at sea, and the captain signed the papers when we returned to Sharne. He then employed me. I made four more voyages with him, and on the fourth I was made first mate when the first mate was killed in a pirate attack. Strange – the pirates were mostly Syrhanese.'

'What happened to the man who was about to slay your captain?' Cleve asked.

Barke shrugged. He waved at the sea. 'Overboard, of course.'

'Of course,' Cleve said, wondering why. 'And how came you to be a prisoner of the Orimors?'

Barke's face clouded and his lips firmed. "I came up this mountain with six others,' he said. 'They were all killed. I am not certain why I was not. Perhaps the Orimors eat people. I think I am a little stringy. I suppose they wanted to fatten me.'

Cleve chuckled, eyeing the other man. Both of them had now stripped to breechclouts and arms belts, retaining their boots. Barke was as muscular as he and a trifle darker. *I come from north of here*, Cleve thought. *That river I was on – it floats from north to south. I'll bet it empties into this ocean!* Yes, Barke would be stringy eating – but more muscular than stringy.

'Why?'

'What? Why what?' Barke asked.

'Why did you and six others climb to the domain of the Orimors?'

Again Barke's face closed in on itself, stormily. 'We came – we went after an Orimor pelt,' he said.

'Should I ask why?'

'No. But I will tell you. Each of us saved the other's life, and there is no debt between us, but our bond will last through all future lives we may live out. I cannot be offended by you, Cleve.' Barke raised his head and gazed at him a moment. 'Although of course it is unlikely that we will see

Chapter Nineteen

The Slave of Sharne

The menacing band of men was uniformed. Each wore a blue-lacquered helmet bound with a scarf of very dark blue. Their tunics were also blue, and their greaves; a shade but a little deeper than that of the Earthly sky. They wore broad, thick belts with enormous buckles, and a baldric whose equally huge buckle was centered on their chests. Strap armor protected their genitals, below a jerkin of black leather that looked capable of turning most sword thrusts. There was a device on the chest, above the heart: shield-shaped, it was a very pale blue field emblazoned with a black sailing ship pierced with a huge curved sword.

Cleve's voice was very quiet: 'Are these men of Sharne?'

'Yes,' Barke muttered.

'Shall I kill them?'

'What?' Barke's voice was incredulous.

'You forget my little box of stone,' Cleve said. The Oridorn sidsorn lay beneath his hand, on the rock beside him.

'No . . . I cannot tell you what to do,' Barke said. 'They will enslave you. Surely I can get out of it.'

Cleve nodded and lifted his hands slowly toward the xenophobic warriors of Sharne, palms out. 'Then I give them the gift of life,' he said.

The leader of the Sharnese stared.

'Whaaat? What's that you say, barbarian?'

'Have you ever heard of Doralan Andrah?' Cleve countered.

'Of course not. And it is I who questions, barbarian.'

'I am not a barbarian. But to answer a question so charmingly put: I told Barke that I give you all the gift of life.'

The man stared at him, his bushy beard writhing as he chewed his lip – or perhaps ground his teeth. 'Good of you. I am always proud to be spared by a man at whose belly are pointed four of my archers' arrows.'

Barke rose to his feet. 'Captain, I am Barke, first mate of *Bluerover.* This man is Cleve of Earth. He saved me from the Orimors, who slew my six companions and took me captive – to eat me, I suppose.'

'Unfortunate. You will be allowed to contact your captain, Citizen Barke. As to your savior . . . you know the law of Sharne.'

'I know it. And I also know he did not speak lightly. He is a sorcerer. He slew an Orimor without a weapon, and without touching him. Look – here are Cleve's clothes.'

The Sharnese captain glanced at the Orimor pelts, then at Cleve. He was frowning, but there was a grudging respect in his eyes. 'How did you slay the Orimor?'

'Orimors,' Cleve corrected. 'Plural. I cannot explain – I would have to show you. Which of your men shall I choose?'

The Sharnese soldiery looked at one another and at their captain.

'Let me feather his belly, Captain,' one of the archers said. 'I think I can do it before he slays me by his magical powers!'

Cleve glanced down. He had risen to his feet, and the source of his sorcery lay on the rock at his feet. He said, 'I have no desire to kill so valiant an archer, Captain, I beg you, deter him from his ridiculous experiment. He will be sinking down dead before his shaft leaves the string, and Daron will not consider this death in battle, surely.

'They do not loose shafts until they're told,' the captain said, and Cleve noticed he was no longer called 'barbarian.'

'What is your business in Sharne, Cleve of – where did Barke say?'

'Earth,' Cleve said. 'And although I dislike telling you my business, I will tell you this: I seek a lady named Lahri. Perhaps you know her.'

'A lady—' The captain definitely blanched. 'I know *of* her,' he said, and he swung his sword down to his left hip, covering the device on his chest with his other hand – the ward sign against sorcery.

Barke was looking strangely at Cleve. Cleve glanced at him, grinned.

'I place myself in your custody, Captain,' Cleve said. 'I am happy to enter Sharne with so fine an escort. There is my sword.' He nodded to the scabbard he had not buckled on after doffing his furry garb. Bending easily, he picked up the sidsorn and slipped it into its pouch on his right hip. He picked up, too, the Oridorn pelts. 'They are still yours,' he muttered to Barke.

Barke drew his sword with his left hand and tossed it at the captain's feet. 'Under protest,' he said, 'and with challenge implied.'

'Oh come, Bluerover Barke! I am but doing my duty as an officer of His Majesty.'

Barke had turned his back to fall in beside Cleve. They made their way with as much dignity as possible down the slope. Their confused captors followed with somewhat less dignity.

'Do you give your parole not to ensorcel, Cleve of Earth?'

Cleve paused at the gateway into the slave pen and turned to face his captor. 'No,' he said. 'I will give it but temporarily, until I see how I am treated and how long I am allowed to remain here. Oh – and until I see how soon Lahri arrives.'

'But—'

Cleve walked into the pen, full of milling people of both sexes. 'You needn't *face* her, Captain,' he called back. 'Merely *send* for her. See whom your courier fears most – you or her!' And Cleve continued walking, into the mass of bodies. The gate slammed behind him.

A citizen suspected of treason, Barke had been taken elsewhere. Cleve had been registered, listened to himself talked about a couple of times, stood aloof during the incredulous stares, and gone precisely where bidden, always as if he were leading or being escorted, rather than being taken. At his hip swung the little pouch bearing the most deadly weapon ever admitted into the color-splashed city of Sharne.

'You just came in,' a pretty girl said; her skin was nearer the color of his own. While of the same race, the Sharnese were in general a little darker than he; he was from the north. Somewhere.

'I did. How long have you been here?'

'Three days,' she said. 'We will all be out tomorrow – tomorrow is market day in Sharne, and we shall be sold. You are a Northman?'

'Uh – well, as opposed to Sharne, yes. I am Cleve of Earth.'

'Earth? I do not know it. I am from Rivshar. You do not look like a slave.' Her brown eyes were huge; her rounded face was framed by a mass of wavy brown hair.

'Neither do you. How many of us here were slaves, a week ago or yesterday or last month?'

She bit her lip. 'I was,' she said. 'I was born a slave. But I offended my mistress, and I am being sold. You are a warrior, and not a slave, and you do not look unkind. Will you do something for me?'

Cleve smiled. 'As much as a slave can do, Rivshar.'

She smiled. 'I am *from* Rivshar. My name is Sovane. Would you stay by me tonight? Some of these men—' She shuddered. 'When the sun goes down, this is a pen of animals. I was twice attacked and taken last night.'

Tears were suddenly as diamonds on her cheek. 'Tomorrow I shall be sold – perhaps to more of the same, but perhaps to someone kind, perhaps to a woman. If only I could sleep in peace tonight . . . without . . . without . . .' Again she shuddered.

He laid a hand on her bare shoulder; she wore a short, loose shift without sleeves. It was torn and dirty, and he thought it strange that it seemed of good cloth, and there was a border about the torn neck he'd have sworn was cloth-of-gold. 'Tonight you will sleep in peace, Sovane. If I am still here.'

She sighed and pushed her shoulder up against his hand. 'I shall be forever indebted,' she said, then her face clouded. 'If you are still here?'

Cleve shrugged. 'I seem to be the first male sorcerer ever seen in Sharne.'

'A sorcerer!' She drew back, her dark eyes wide.

'Sh – Let's not cause a furor among our fellow slaves,' he told her.

'But – why did you allow them to take you? Why are you in here? Fly away, or something.'

'If I do, Sovane, I will try to take you with me. But – I cannot, not yet. I have given my parole. We will see.' He looked about.

The enormous pen was filled with men and women of all ages; indeed, some were only children. A few were with a parent or parents, others were alone; frightened, abandoned animals waiting to be sold into servitude in the city whose king called himself ruler of the world. They were clothed in shifts, in tunics, in breechclouts, and many were not clothed at all. Some had been here for six days; some a few hours. There was a weekly auction, so that only those who were not bought spent more than six days here.

'And what,' Cleve asked, 'if they are not bought on the second trip to the block?'

Sovane shivered. 'That depends upon their age or health,' she said, 'though most of those not sold are old or ill or crippled. They are either sent to the mines, or . . . killed.'

'Which is worse?' he asked thoughtfully, and she shook her head.

'I am not sure.'

'Sovane . . . your shift has got itself dirty and torn here, but – it isn't the material one expects to find on slaves. Where were you yesterday?'

She looked at the ground; dust, beneath their feet. 'In the palace. I have been a slave there since my birth. I was sixteen when I was given to Selka on her eighteenth birthday, last year.'

'Selka?'

She looked up at him, unbelieving. 'You don't know? Earth *is* a far land! Sharnan Selka is daughter of Sharnan Vreen and Sharnan Kelas, his queen. Selka is Princess of Sharne.'

'And intensely cruel and spoiled, and you're here because of some trifling incident.'

Her big brown eyes looked up into his. She shook her head

with a wistful smile. 'She is a fine lady, my mist – my former mistress. And my crime was serious enough – the queen found me with Prince Reven. I did not want to be there – how does one refuse to tarry with the prince-heir of Sharne? At any rate, Queen Kelas screeched and slapped both of us, and he fled. Then she ordered me brought here at once. Princess Selka does not even know where I am. Nor does the prince.'

'Her mother wouldn't tell her?'

Again she gave him the incredulous look from her pretty little face. 'Know, Cleve of Earth, what I am sure many of the people of Sharne know: It is Queen Kelas who holds the supreme power, because King Vreen is scared of her – she is a Starpowered One he brought here from Syrhane. She in her turn hates him, I think, and her daughter, too, for Princess Selka should have inherited her powers but did not. Too, Selka is a lady, and kind, as I said. The queen loves only herself – and her son, who at least looks like her. She will do something terrible to the king someday, and rule even more firmly than she does now, through Prince Reven. She has her lovers, Her Majesty has, but poor Reven must not. She is saving him for a Starpowered One.' Sovane looked sad.

'Somewhat confusing,' Cleve admitted, 'but not too unfamiliar a situation. You haven't of course heard of Catherine the Great. . . . Well, what have we now? Is that man motioning to me?'

'Oh! he is! And that's her carriage!'

'Kelas?'

'No! Karikal Lahri, Witch of Karikal!'

'Good!' Cleve grasped her little hand, grinning. 'Come along, Sovane of Rivshar.'

'No – please!' She hung back, straining to free her arm, clutching and pulling at his wrist with the other hand.

'Stop that, Sovane. I will not leave here without you – unless you'd rather stay. I think there's at least one who'd rather you did – that big fellow over there, the one with the off-eye who needs a haircut. He's been watching us ever since I came in.'

She took one look at the naked man he indicated and

shrank against him. The off-eyed man grinned, leering. 'Oh, no, no . . . he is one of the two who . . .'

'So I thought. Come along.'

Nearly pulling his unwilling little friend, who was uncertain which to fear most – Lahri of Karikal or her ravisher of the night before – Cleve strode to the fence surrounding the slave pen. Drawn up beside it was a sedan chair of unrelieved black, carried by four equally black men of heroic physique and shorn heads. As they approached, Cleve saw that the men's skins had been stained: they were of his own race. It occurred to him that he did not know if there were black men on Andor or not. He did know there were white; Oridorna and Orisana represented the only true white races he was ever likely to see.

Beside the slavemaster stood a tall, thin man in a black robe. His head was bald; his eyes blue and cold as a polar sea.

'Are you Cleve of Earth?'

'I am.'

'Are you a sorcerer?'

'You could say that.'

'Do not answer me thus, I asked if you are a sorcerer. Are you the man who slays without touching and without weapons – notably Orimors?'

Cleve nodded. 'That,' he said, 'I am.'

The tall, thin man turned to the slavemaster. 'This man,' he said, 'is purchased by the Witch of Karikal. Send us your bill.'

'Wait,' Cleve said. He half-turned, bringing forth the girl trying to hide behind him. 'Sovane of Rivshar comes with me.'

'Oh, my lord,' the slavemaster said. '*That* one! Why, she is a valuable prize, a virgin from—'

'He lies,' Cleve said. 'There are no such in this pen. I am sure our slavemaster separates them out – for those who enter as maidens leave as women.' He glared at the slavemaster.

The man blanched and opened his mouth to curse.

'Silence,' the tall man in the black robe said, and the slavemaster's mouth closed. Cleve was sure he'd have heard the click were it not for the noise of the slaves behind him. 'You are bought, Cleve of Earth, but if you do not offer proof of your claim you will be on the block tomorrow. By what power do you dare tell me this girl comes with you?'

'By the power of Louisville,' Cleve said. 'By the powers of the star Sol, and America, and Washington-Adams-Jefferson-Madison-Monroe-Adams. By the power that slays Orimors from a distance, without weapons.'

The tall, bald man stared at him. His thin moustache and beard twitched.

A black curtain was drawn back on the palanquin behind him, by a slim hand wearing a black ring. 'Zamph!' a female voice hissed from the sedan chair; nothing of her showed save her slender fingers. 'Cease this wrangling chatter! Bring them both, before Starpowered Cleve sends you ahead to a life less easy than this one!'

The tall, bald man stiffened. He nodded. 'We buy them both,' he snapped. 'Send us your bill, slavemaster, and be careful of it – you know the buyer! Now, open that gate and release them!'

A few moments later, Cleve and the shrinking girl walked out of the slave pen of Sharne.

Chapter Twenty

The Witch of Sharne

She was neither tall nor short; neither so slender as Siraa of Orisana nor plump; neither a girl nor an old woman. She was a medium-built woman of medium height, classically featured in cold, handsome dignity rather than pretty or what is usually thought of as attractive. Her eyes were blue, pale blue, like thick ice on a winter's day. They were set in a face so pale it abruptly, curiously reminded Cleve of those within White Mountain, after his day among the sun-bronzed people of Sharne. All the more pale by contrast with her hair; the hair all the more striking in its rich walnut coloration by contrast to her strangely fair skin. It was drawn up atop her head, twisted high and laced with pearls from the rich beds of Sharne's shores. It grew down into a widow's peak; in front of her ears it had been made to curl forward on her cheeks in loops that fell just short of closing. Her nose was straight and thin; aristocratic. The bones of her head, her austere face, were finely, sharply molded. Thick, dark brows grew in a straight line above her eyes; they were long, narrow eyes, well shuttered.

She looked like anything but Robert Cleve's concept of a witch. The term 'sorceress' was better, he thought, in the language of Earth; it evoked images of this sort of attractive, tempting woman, rather than of crones in peaked caps with warts on chin and nose.

'I am Lahri, Witch of Karikal, called Witch of Sharne. My brother Zamph brought you here. You are Cleve of Earth, who slays unarmed and from a distance, who exchanges words with invisible or vanishing comrades, who causes Orimor corpses to vanish, who rescued Bluerover Barke – while wearing a suit sewn of Orimor pelts.'

'You know much more of me than I of you, Witch of Karikal. I thank you for being taken from that pen of poor destitutes . . . before I was forced to demonstrate my powers.'

Lahri smiled. 'And what are your powers, Cleve of Earth? Will you have wine?'

'You have named my powers,' he told her, his eyes moving about the sumptuous apartment. Only when the witch had again intervened with her solemn word, had Cleve agreed to leave Sovane outside while he entered to this audience. 'And yes, I will join you in wine.'

'Show me,' she said. She raised and swung one arm as she snapped her fingers, the long, loose sleeve of her black gown flapping. It was banded and bordered with silver, the robe that fit her like wrinkle-free skin above its sash and to her svelte hips, falling broad and loose from there to the floor. At the hem, silver-lacquered toenails peeped from the ends of silver sandals.

'Show you? Would you have me slay you, Witch of Karikal?'

She smiled her thin-lipped smile. 'You cannot kill me.'

'Then I cannot show you,' he shrugged. He was very aware of being sweaty and underdressed, in this magnificent apartment of black and silver and scarlet – the deep carpet beneath his feet – and in the presence of his regally attired hostess.

Again Lahri smiled; it was slow and restrained, her smile; far from effervescent. She was very, very sure of herself, confident with power so certain, it was casually held. She nodded; his head turned in the indicated direction.

The girl, bouncy and rippling of breast and plump of belly and bottom, wore a ridiculously low orange skirt supported by two thin, black straps that crossed on both her back and chest between the jiggling halves of her bare bosom. She entered with quick, flatfooted steps, bearing a carafe and goblets on a small salver. Her eyes were directed floorward.

'Her, then,' Lahri said in a casual tone.

Fascinated by the girl, Cleve jerked his eyes and his attention back to the seated sorceress. 'I beg your pardon?'

'I asked you to show me your power. Use her.' She tilted her head at the girl without looking at her; the girl was filling the silver goblets from the silver carafe.

'No,' Cleve said. He accepted his wine with a smile at the slave Lahri seemed to consider so expendable. 'Thank you.'

Lahri cocked her head to gaze at him. 'No? You refuse?'

'Of course I refuse.'

'Why? That—' again she jerked her head '– is only a slave.'

'That,' Cleve said, wishing she would sip her wine so that he could quench his thirst with the lovely amber liquid, 'is a human being.'

'She is a slave!'

Cleve smiled. 'I remind my gracious hostess that in Sharne, all but Sharnese are considered slaves. I was in the slave pens when my lady Lahri first saw me. How many artisans, cooks, poets, engineers, even physicians are in that animal pen? This girl had parents, who loved and she was born. Surely she has intelligence. Even barring that, she serves well and is most pleasant to look upon. Reason enough not to destroy her.' He stood flatfooted, holding the chased goblet in his left hand, and his gaze met Lahri's directly.

She stared at him; her slave had departed as silently as she had entered, through a tall paneled door that closed with a muted *thump* behind her wriggly backside.

'You are a *man*,' Lahri said. 'Had you started to slay her, I'd have stopped you. You are a human being in a world of beastly slaves.' Suddenly she frowned. 'Who – are – you?'

'Has my lady of Karikal ever heard the name Doralan Andrah?'

'Doralan? A clan unknown to me. No, I cannot recognize the name Andrah, either. It has a most foreign flavor. Where—' Frowning, she bent forward, her pale-eyed gaze very intent. '*You* are Doralan Andrah! But also Cleve . . . Robert Cleve? From . . . another *world*!' Her eyes had widened; her reserve faltered. 'And you know not where Doralan Andrah is from!' She sat well forward, her hands tight-clutched on the arms of her black-lacquered chair. 'How is it that you are two men in one body?'

'I – hm. I have not shown you my power, Karikal Lahri, but you have just demonstrated your own.'

She smiled. 'Yes. I can tell you no more now,' she said,

rather sadly. 'But yes. I see into minds. Tell me – are you in truth a sorcerer?'

'Please taste your wine,' Cleve said. 'I am suffering from thirst.' He waited until she had sipped, perfunctorily; her mind was on him, and his mind, and she was uninterested in the fruit of Andorite vines. He drank deeply. 'Thank you. No, I am no sorcerer. I may have powers here – if I can implement my knowledge from that other world you see in my mind.'

'I thought as much,' she said, gazing intently at him. 'But I do not see; I saw. It comes in flashes, Cleve.'

'Are you a sorceress?'

She stared, then laughed. 'Oh gods, oh gods! An intelligent man, and daring! How long since anyone has dared to say anything even approaching that to me – and you practically ordered me to drink, too . . . because you are too mannerly to drink before your host! What a strange mixture you are, Cleve! How many mixtures!'

'You did not answer,' he said quietly. 'I think you are not a sorceress at all. You are a handsome woman, very confident, with a power granted to few on any world, in any time: You can hear thoughts within the minds of other persons. That alone is power – if the possessor is clever, and highly intelligent.'

Her laugh was a silvery sound like water over rocks sparkling in the sun. 'An intelligent man, and daring! There is not one in Sharne. All hold me in awe, and few think. Our rules claim dominion over a world we have not begun to explore, because we are surely the greatest maritime power in the world. And to see you, to have that glimpse of your *mind*! A moving, working, crystal vision, rather than the murk and fog I am accustomed to. It swirls in the mind of our king . . . ruler of the World!' Her voice was scoffing; a sharp-edged weapon he knew she kept fine-honed. 'And the slaying of the Orimors?' she asked.

'I have a weapon,' he told her. He resisted the impulse to pat the pouch on his left hip. 'It is dangerous to others. There were other men with me; they – have power. They took the bodies and – left.'

She nodded, leaning slowly back. A lonely woman, a witch who was not a witch, not a Starpowered One, but who had so used her gift that she was feared and respected and kowtowed to like some ancient Chinese empress. On Earth she'd be written of in the newspapers, perhaps with her own column, called from place to place to demonstrate that which set her apart and made her a freak – alone and apart. Here she used that ability, similarly, but with more dignity. And still it set her apart, as she had probably wanted, in the beginning. Now she had achieved her goals – and learned of the loneliness that goes with high intelligence or an unusual gift. And certainly with both of them combined.

And she had found her intellectual peer. Cleve gazed at her, a woman a very few years his senior; she was perhaps thirty, perhaps twenty-nine or thirty-one.

'I wonder now if the queen is a witch,' he said. 'You have answered me with your silence – which I shall keep.'

'I believe you will,' Lahri said. 'It doesn't matter though. Go about Sharne saying that Karikal Lahri is not a witch, and you will be laughed at – and probably killed, by some groveling, mindless worm of a man who will come here to tell me how he has proved his devotion. But – yes, Her Majesty is a witch; a Starpowered One, and dangerous. I will tell you this: I am not dangerous to you, Robert Cleve.'

He bowed his head with a little smile, trying to show at once gratitude and unconcern. He succeeded; again he heard the lovely, bubbling sound of her laughter.

'You are concealing something,' Lahri said, 'and I shall not probe after it. Your friends on the mountain . . . if the Witch of Karikal promises only goodwill and silence, will you tell her your history?'

Cleve drank again. He stood on the soft crimson carpet before her, breechclouted and barefoot, since his Orimor-fur boots were with the rest of the coldsuit he'd given Barke. 'Your pardon, my lady of Karikal, but . . . what do I know of the word, the promises of the Witch of Sharne?'

She regarded him in astonished silence, her gaze as much one of wonder as of astonishment. 'You tell me straight out – couched in pretty words, but straight out, nonetheless –

that you don't trust me! Do you know that men have died for much less?'

'I have no doubt of it,' Cleve said, smiling a tight smile.

Again she cocked her head. Her austerity gave way to a whimsical smile, almost girlish. 'Cleve, Cleve? Or Doralan ... what shall we do? We fence with one another to no avail, yet we are each fascinated with the other, and each of us knows he can be of value, one to the other.'

'How can I be of value to you, Lahri of Karikal?'

'Shall I tell you?' Her eyes sparkled with girlish fervor. Then she said quietly, 'You are a man, and I meet few. I remember one, six years ago ... You can be of value to me by taking dinner with me, by talking with me, by sitting up far into the night and drinking wine as we talk.'

His brows were up. 'And how can the Witch of Karikal be of value to me?'

She half-rose, her knuckles white on the carved arms of her chair, her face tightening with the anger that turned her eyes dangerously scintillant, cold as the northern ice they resembled. 'Don't push me too far, Cleve/Andrah!'

'You are oversensitive, from years of being treated as a queen – by those for whom you feel only contempt. Make up your mind, Lahri.'

She sank slowly back, again with astonishment and wonder in her eyes – and respect, and admiration, and perhaps ... 'My value to you? You are here, not in the slave pen. You do not know where you are from, *Doralan Andrah*, or where you are going, because – you have been ensorceled! Do you not know that dark powers granted by the stars themselves have robbed you of your memory?'

Cleve stared at her. He felt as if he'd been struck forcibly just below the sternum by a great, ice-gloved hand.

'And ... you can ...'

She nodded. 'Of course. Memories can be transferred, or locked, but never do they leave the skull of their first possessor. Yours have merely been locked up in a corner of your mind and the door closed and locked against you.' She smiled. 'But not, I think, against me.'

'I think it is past time you invited me to sit,' he said.

'I've been waiting for you to assert yourself there, too. Please sit down, Cleve of Earth, Doralan of . . . someplace.'

He sank down onto a chair; hers was tall, and padded, and set to face the door like a throne in which she rested to greet and doubtless strike dumb and fearful all visitors.

'What is your price?'

'My price, Cleve of Earth?' Slowly her smile widened. Her serene self-possession was returning; she was again in control, and she knew it. 'You must perform a service for me, a mission that will take you not far and present little danger. It will take nearly a month.'

He pursed his mouth. 'To know that I am going to know all of it, all that I've forgotten . . . and to have to wait a month. No – I will agree if it can be done simultaneously, my mission for you and your opening of my mind's dark corner.'

She nodded. 'Exactly!'

'I agree, then. Must I climb the mountain for an Orimor pelt?'

'Oh, Cleve! I told you it was nothing so dangerous! Nor must you leave this house. It is as I said: Dine with me, talk with me, sit late at night drinking wine and talking, that each of us might share an intelligent mind for a while.'

It seemed a strange phrase to apply to one so queenly, but it was the best he could think of. There was *mischief* in her clear, pale eyes.

'That girl, the one you insisted on bringing from the slave pen,' Lahri said. 'Why?'

And he knew. He lifted his shoulders. 'A whim. She seems a sweet enough child. The queen caught the prince with her, and sold her at once. She was twice used last night, and I promised her my protection. If I had left without her, I'd have failed to honor my promise – too, I'd have raised her hopes and then shattered them. She's had enough such blows, I think.'

Karikal Lahri studied him, and once more her eyes were near-invisible with those long, slitted lids. 'I do believe you are telling the truth,' she said, shaking her head. 'Extraordinary! Do you always honor your promises?'

He did, and he did all in his power to put nothing else in his mind, to broadcast the thought, as he told her, 'I try.'

'You do; your thoughts just flashed in my mind again. Well, then. We have a bargain. You will want a bath, and some clothing, and then we will sit down and sup together, Doralan Andrah. And then we shall go about learning who Doralan Andrah is.'

Doralan Andrah nodded. He arose and went to be groomed.

Chapter Twenty-One

The Memory of Doralan

For the greater part of an Andorite month – twenty-eight days, the cycle of the nearer moon and of Andorite women – Robert Cleve tarried in Sharne with Karikal Lahri, and he shared her table and his warmth, and they enjoyed each other's company to the fullest. He felt he knew what she wanted, this lonely, childless woman who'd found no man worthy, and he hoped sincerely that she knew what she was about and would indeed have, in nine months, something to show for her bargain with him; something other than the memories she would keep always, to recall and cherish. As he would.

Lahri farmed out Barke's request and pelts to a lesser witch – a genuinely Starpowered One, Lahri pointed out, who if she but knew, could remove the Witch of Karikal from the world in a trice with one simple spell. She reported back, that second witch: The deed was done, though Lahri would not tell her guest of Barke's request; it was a professional secret, she told him, and tumbled back laughing on silken sheets.

Her black-garbed brother treated Cleve with the utmost respect, and Cleve saw nothing in the man's eyes to indicate enmity toward his sister's conquest. Only Zamph went abroad; Lahri's paleness of skin came from her never venturing out of her palatial home, save within the curtained palanquin carried by the four huge black men. It aided her image, she told him, as he had not needed to be told.

She set two 'lesser' witches to work on his problem, and sought to solve it herself via the simple road of hypnotism and telepathy. She caught only fleeting sparkles of his lost knowledge, but one night, the twenty-first, he woke from a sleep that had grown increasingly troublous. He sat suddenly erect in bed, his eyes wide in the darkness.

He was Doralan Andrah, the Doralan of Doralan, Grof of

Mor and of the allied clans of Elgain, and thus Morgrof of Elgain. He saw Biyah, and mighty Stek, and the clan chiefs, and he saw the smiling Witch of Khoramor and her ambitious brother. He saw a time when the night was dark and alive with a thousand natural scents, his room darkened and beautiful with draperies and carved panels and filled with the mingled redolences of incense and perfumes and many flowers. A night of romance and necromancy, a night of Doralan Andrah and Khoramor Shansi. He remembered, feeling it again, and he remembered dozing, overwhelmed with fatigue. And then he remembered waking naked and without Andorite memory, on that raft abroad on Sky River.

'What – what is it, my love?' a voice asked; the voice of another witch, another enchantress, one who also possessed a brother, but whose ambitions were far more womanly and far more noble and far less consequent – to the world, though not to herself – than Khoramor Shansi's.

Cleve told her.

In the moonslight striding boldly through the window, he saw a tear, a single, glistening tear, on Lahri's pale cheek.

'It is done, then, and not through me – an enchantment of one of the others of Sharne has taken effect to overcome your old ensorcelment.

'Yes,' he murmured, touching her small and very feminine shoulder. 'Tell me, Lahri – did you really try?'

She threw her arms around him; he was hard and muscular and trembling with the return of a lifetime of memories, rushing back like a great tidal wave engulfing the shores of his mind in the darkness . . . the darkness that no longer shrouded his brain.

'Oh, Cleve! Oh, my lord! I have tried, I have tried! I swear to you, I swear to it. Beat me, trample me, but don't doubt me.'

He patted her quivering back. 'I do not doubt you, Lahri,' he told her. 'You still haven't learned to know insults from jests – it comes from having been too long a queenly sorceress! But – hush. Sit back, and let me tell you who I am, what I am, and how I came here.'

She sat back to gaze at him in the moonlit dark. Her face

was nearly invisible to him, save where the moon kissed her left cheek.

He paced the room. 'I must get back there. Elgain cannot be reached by sea. I know where it lies from the sea, but as Doralan Andrah, I've never seen it. I can draw a map, and fill it with what I know now, as Cleve, although I've little idea of distances. I know who set me out on Sky River, who took my memories in the night, and I know how she accomplished it. I was warned! As to the rest of it, the exact how and what she did, and how long ago – no, there I am blank, for I was unconscious.'

'A witch?'

He nodded. 'Khoramor Shansi. Her brother Shant was my rival for the throne of Mor in Elgain. I believe she desired that power more than he, although I can't imagine either of them holding the clans together. Oh, God – what's happened there now? What, after my disappearance? What of the Clan Doralan?'

'She loved you? You love her? You gave her something of yourself?' Lahri's voice was soft and tiny in the darkness.

'That last, yes, in a moment of perfumed insanity. But love? No, there was none of that, not on either side. She's a temptress, my love, even as you are. But with purpose far more devious – don't think I don't know yours. She set out to entrance me and I succumbed willingly, though warned. Oh, I was warned! Doralan Andrah's memory knew, but I could not bring myself to believe in sorcery other than natural science, despite his memories. No, Lahri, there was no love.'

Realizing her hurt and her fear, realizing what had dictated her question, he went to her and cupped her shoulders in his big hands.

'Only infatuation, and a falling. There was no such love as we have, Lahri.'

And again she hurled herself against him, straining close. She was stifling the sound of her sobs, but he felt them quaking her body.

'Is it done, Lahri?'

'What?' She spoke against him, her face hard-pressed to his strength.

'You know. I must leave. I wish I could leave tonight. But there's our bargain, too – is it accomplished?'

She sighed, still trembling with inner sobs, and he remembered, abruptly and without meaning to, the tearless girl named Jaire, who saw with her mouth and her throat as Lahri saw – sometimes – with her mind.

'I . . . think so,' she said. 'How can I be sure, yet? But – the time is past.' Her voice was quiet, sad, a girl's voice, disappointed but resigned. She released him and sat back, her legs tucked up, her knees peeking from her gown. She gazed up at him. Now his face was invisible, while he could see hers in the moonslight; he had circled the room in his restless excitement, to stand with his back to the window.

'I signed the papers the day after you arrived and sent them to the magistrate,' she told him. 'You were never a slave, of course, but in Sharne . . . I 'freed' you, and have the papers for you. Thus, you can leave here as a free man. As to the method – I shall have Barke here in the morning. *Bluerover*'s captain has died of pneumonia, but not before telling the owner Barke should succeed him. The owner lost no time clearing Barke of that ridiculous conspiracy charge. He is master of *Bluerover* now. You and he can work out a course of action.'

He touched her arm. 'You,' he said. 'You thought of it all.'

Her fingers wrapped around his wrist. There is nothing you can do tonight, of course.'

'No . . . no, of course not.'

Her fingers tightened. 'Then come back to me now. If it is a week before you leave, we will say good-bye again and again, every night.'

Chapter Twenty-Two

The Dungeon of Sharne

The horsemen from the palace arrived next morning not ten minutes after Lahri's messenger had departed to bring Barke. Zamph came in with the word, worry in his normally cold eyes; he worked hard at playing the role of major-domo to the Witch of Karikal. The men from the palace were the Queen's Own, and they wanted the man Cleve, of Earth.

Lahri mirrored his frown. 'For what purpose?'

'An audience with Her Majesty,' her brother told them.

Cleve rose. 'I can't imagine why Her Majesty wants to talk with an Outlander, and worse, a Northman, and worse, a freedman,' he said, smiling. 'But one doesn't refuse royal invitations, does one?'

They shook their heads. Lahri came to him.

'Be careful, Andrah.'

Cleve nodded, and kissed her, and left. As he crossed the anteroom, the tall, bald man grasped his arm from behind. Cleve paused.

'Andrah heed her. Be very careful. Remember that Queen Kelas rules Sharne, and that she is Starpowered.'

Cleve turned to him with a genuine smile. He gripped the austere man's forearm. 'Thank you, Zamph! I'll be careful.'

The leader of the troop of six horsemen had dismounted to stand waiting outside, one jackbooted foot on the steps. The camailed helmets and gleaming blue-stained leather cuirasses over white tunics and thigh-length black boots made an impressive showing, Cleve thought, squinting in the bright sunlight. How they must suffer from the heat! Her Majesty had thought of show rather than the wearer's comfort, in designing the uniforms for her Queen's Own Corps.

'Doralan Andrah of . . .'

'Elgain,' Cleve said proudly; at last he had both name and nationality on Andor!

'Elgain? I have not heard of it.'

'Sergeant, this is going to hurt,' Cleve told him, descending the steps. 'But in Elgain we have never heard of Sharne. Is this horse for me?'

'Of course,' the sergeant said, with a sour expression. Cleve was right; no Sharne cared to hear what he'd just said. 'Do you ride?'

Cleve ignored him, mounting the bluegray beast with its ground-trailing tail and long mane of far paler gray. The animal rippled its floppy ears and tossed its big head as Cleve took up the reins.

'Follow us,' the sergeant said as he swung up.

'I'll ride beside you,' Cleve told him. He had no desire to eat their dust and see nothing but the handsome flapping cloaks they wore. 'I was invited, was I not? You're not arresting me?'

'Correct,' the sergeant said shortly, and his horse shot forward. Cleve quickly reined up beside him. They rode through the colorful city in silence, the sergeant's detail following.

The palace was all pomp and hustle-bustle and fancy clothes; everywhere stood sword-girt guards with helmets that revealed only their eyes and mouths, halberds held stiffly beside their right boots. Berobed dignitaries – for in the palace, in the employ of those who called themselves rulers of the world, even freedmen and slaves were dignitaries – moved rapidly here and there, looking very important.

Cleve was prepared to be kept waiting, and was thus amazed to be ushered in to the Presence by a very fat, bald man in a yellow robe resplendent with pearls and purple embroidery. He made introductions. Cleve was 'Cleve of Earth,' and Queen Kelas, 'Andorgroffe.'

Two stony-faced guards with spiked helmets and short pikes flanked the Queen of Sharne, a big, round-faced woman of forty or so years. So berobed and encrusted with gold and pearls and stiff cloth-of-gold and jewels was she that Cleve had little idea of her figure beneath her trappings, mostly gold and the deep blue-green of the sea. Big, he thought, and overweight, particularly in the chest.

'And where is Elgain?' she asked crisply, seeking to pierce and intimidate him with a very keen gaze from dark eyes. She sat on a well-padded chair two steps above the floor; it was of tesselated tile, off-white and sea-blue.

He had anticipated that question. Elgain, he knew, was at the foot of the Mountains of Mist, near the headwaters of Sky River. It was far northwest of Sharne, inland and thus nearly inaccessible; the long range of the White Mountains effectively bisected the hemisphere, east and west. He assumed one could reach Elgain by sailing from Sharne, on the southeast coast, northward to Rivshar, and then marching inland. Or by marching west until one reached Sky River, and following it north. He had no idea how far; he did not know how long he'd lain unconscious on his raft.

He answered truthfully, if incompletely. 'I am not sure, Your Majesty. I was ensorceled and set adrift, naked and unarmed.'

'Um. Thus you sought out a sorceress when you came here ... what is Elgain's population?'

He had not the foggiest notion. He did know that Sharne claimed seven hundred thousand, and he thought it wise to say, 'Something over five hundred thousand, Your Majesty.'

'Surely no place is so populous!' she said, her very keen eyes showing her surprise.

'Your pardon. Perhaps I am wrong.'

A smile almost succeeded in drawing back the corner of her purpled mouth. 'You are clever, and bold. I do not believe you, in any of this. How came you here?'

'As I said, I was ensorceled and set adrift by enemies. I assure Your Majesty she would not believe how I came to be in Sharne. You must know that when your Citizen Barke met me, I was descending this side of White Mountain.' He could not resist adding, 'I left a marker on the peak, with my name.'

She studied his face, frowning, but yes, he knew that she already had that story. Why was she so interested? Because he'd been nearly a month in the Karikal mansion? 'You crossed the White Range?'

He smiled. 'I assured Your Majesty my story would not be

believable,' he said, allowing her to think what she might. He would not offer Sharne a fresh source of slaves by telling her of the people inside the mountains whose peaks loomed tall above her city-state. Sharne was a proud and haughty and arrogant land; with the Oridorn sidsorns they'd soon be on their way to world domination. Another Rome.

She spoke crisply: 'If I say that I believe none of it, you will smile and say, "That is Your Majesty's privilege," or something similar, because you are a clever adventurer. We trade with Rivshar, and know that there are no civilized peoples among the Northlands. And the White Range is not crossable.' She shrugged a broad, meaty shoulder. 'It matters little to me: I am lied to constantly. You are here to tell me the whereabouts of a certain Riv slavegirl, who left the slave pen with you nearly a period ago. She has not been seen since, nor is there a record of sale or writ of manumission, although I signed yours.'

She was not interested in him at all! She had meant to watch the girl Sovane of Rivshar, send spies to see who bought her, perhaps have her bought and either slain or shipped out on the first far-bound vessel. And she had lost her, and her only interest in him was the whereabouts of little Sovane of Rivshar! But – what should he tell her? Would it protect Sovane if he told Queen Kelas that her quarry was in the home of the Witch of Karikal? – or would that only endanger Lahri as well as Sovane? What would Lahri do if the Queen's Own arrived, demanding the girl?

Cleve thought about that, and he did not want to find out; he feared Lahri would act as the Witch of Sharne, and only did this woman before him possess Starpower; she was queen.

'She'd been attacked in the night,' he said, 'and I promised her protection in the pens. So I brought her when I left. Then we became separated. I had no deep personal interest in her.' All of which was true. He did not know exactly where Sovane was at this moment, somewhere happily within Lahri's walls, and he had indeed been separated from her there, at both his and Lahri's wish.

'I believe absolutely nothing you have told me,' the woman

with the deep-seeing eyes said. 'You are Cleve of Earth, but there is no such place. You tricked Barke, who was delirious with shock and cold. You have enchanted the enchantress Lahri, which I can understand – you are handsome and muscular and far from unintelligent. And you have secreted that scheming little slave-girl somewhere. You will rest here, Northman, until you decide which is more valuable – that girl, or the rest of your life. For it will be spent within four close stone walls underground unless you decide to speak up! Guards!'

Cleve considered taking them then, with the little weapon resting unobtrusively on right hip; the guards had taken his sword, but had not examined a pouch too small to contain a dagger. He did not. He allowed himself to be led along a corridor and down some steps. They crossed a landing past a barred door that led outside. There was another door, and he waited as it was unlocked and unchained. Stale, chill air swirled up to smite his nostrils. Beyond, he saw darkness, and stone steps, leading down. The dungeons of Sharne!

He never saw them. One of his two jailers was at the door; the other stood at Cleve's left elbow. Cleve calmly opened the pouch, took out the little stone box, and slipped his thumb into the loop. The man at the door looked up.

'Here, what're you doing? What's that thing?' And his hand flashed across his belly to his sword hilt.

Cleve watched the man's chest blacken around the hole that appeared suddenly in it. His cry chocked off as he staggered back, then toppled and rolled down the steps into the dungeon. Cleve leaped to his right, twisting. The other Sharnese was just scraping his sword out of its sheath. Cleve raised the sidsorn and triggered it again, and the man gasped and died with a growing hole at the base of his throat.

Hanging onto the sidsorn that had just slain two men so quickly and silently, Cleve dragged the dead soldier over to the doorway leading below. He took the man's sword before thrusting him through the doorway and listening to the body thump and scrape and rattle down the long stair. Cleve slammed the door, replaced the chain, and closed the big lock. The key was still in the grasp of the first dead jailer.

Swinging to the door leading outside, Cleve peered out. Interesting; it seemed to be the same . . . and he remembered. He'd seen the palace from the mountain slope that day with Barke – it was Y-shaped. He and his escort had ridden into the courtyard just at the intersection of the Y, entered near the center of one arm. And then walked here – he was at the intersection again. Outside stood the horse he'd ridden here from Karikal House!

Sheathing his new sword, he unbarred the door and hurried out of the palace. His pace slowed once he was away from the door. He nodded politely to a pair of passing soldiers – the king's, he supposed; they were not *hers* – and nodded again to the slave standing near the horses. The man said nothing, watching as Cleve swung up and reined the animal about.

'Uh – are you not being escorted back?' the man asked. 'You came in with several of the Queen's Own—'

Cleve flashed him a broad grin with a touch of ruefulness in it. 'I am not so important as Her Majesty thought,' he said, and for a moment they smiled at each other, two men touched by power but untroubled by its possession.

Then Cleve swung the animal and made for the gate.

Just as he passed through – without question; one encountered more difficulty entering than leaving official premises – he met an approaching horseman.

'Cleve!'

'Barke!' Cleve spoke rapidly, quietly. 'I am fleeing. I was condemned to the dungeon. I killed two guards and locked them down there. So far, no one knows. I can't endanger Lahri by returning there – tell me where I can go.'

'To the docks,' Barke said; the man certainly had no trouble with fast thinking! '*Bluerover*'s easy to spot: blue hull, blue sails. The ring I gave you will get you aboard. Stay below, and I'll see you tonight.'

Barke paced his mount on past, to be accosted by the guards; the quiet exchange between him and Cleve had taken perhaps forty seconds.

Cleve made his way to the harbor as fast as he could without endangering pedestrians or calling attention to himself.

Bluerover was indeed easy to recognize, the man barring his way did indeed recognize the iron ring – laughing – and soon Cleve was below, raiding the wine cabinet in the captain's cabin.

Chapter Twenty-Three

The Spells of Sharne

There was only blackness outside the port of the Sharnese merchantman *Bluerover* when Barke entered. He and Cleve gripped forearms, grinning in the darkness. Barke lit a lamp. After several false starts, Cleve convinced him to pour wine and tell a coherent story.

Barke admitted that his quest up White Mountain had been insanity, but he was insane, he said – in love, certainly not a rational state. A spell was required for him to win his 'Sulky.' Barke went to Lahri. After a two-day wait (while she conferred with a 'lesser' witch capable of solving the problem, Cleve mused), Lahri told Barke that an Orimor pelt would be necessary for the spell he craved. He ascended White Mountain, was captured, rescued by Cleve, and returned to be accused of conspiracy. Then *Bluerover*'s captain died, naming Barke as his choice of successor, and the ship's owner implemented both Barke's acquittal and promotion.

His first voyage, up the coast to Rivshar, was scheduled for six days hence. Meanwhile, other matters had gone his way – apparently the Orimor pelt was successful, for he'd won his lady.

'We must flee Sharne, Cleve. Sulky's parents don't know, and they'd never approve. Captain of *Bluerover* or not, I'm a foreign freedman. I arrived at Karikal House this morning just after you left for your interview with the queen. Naturally I agreed to Karikal Lahri's idea – that I take both you and Sulky with me when I sail. I was on my way to the palace to wait for you when I met you at the gate. Her Majesty did some spelling this afternoon, and came out white-faced. You seem to represent a terrible danger to the entire royal family of Sharne, Cleve. She yelled several times, "I'll lose my children through him if that man isn't destroyed!" That is when they discovered your escape – hours after you effected it. Clever of you to be so neat about it – both guards dead and in the dungeon, and the door chained and locked!'

Cleve smiled a quiet smile, waiting for the rest.

'We shall merely have to sail a few days early,' Barke said. 'They're scouring the city for you. My love will be along soon. We'll be short-crewed, I'm afraid, and you and she may well have to help on deck, poor girl.'

Cleve shook his head. 'Dangerous – smuggling me out of Sharne is the wrong way to start a honeymoon!' At least he thought of it as 'honeymoon'; the Sharnese term was 'love-night.' The people of Andor had not yet civilized themselves out of frankness in most matters.

'Look here, Cleve or Doralan sire, whichever I'm to call you—'

'Andrah, I suppose,' Cleve said.

'Um. Andrah, then. I cannot stay in Sharne. Every time she and I see each other, we're in danger – especially me! We've already talked of fleeing, planned for it. Naturally, we knew we could never return. We planned to just disappear in Rivshar. This way, perhaps we can all go to . . . is it Elgain?'

'It is,' Cleve smiled. 'But I can't guarantee welcome. I am not certain of *my* reception there. I've no doubt my rival and his witch-sister now rule or try to. All right, then, Barke. When do we sail?'

'Sooner than I care to, and I hope you had a good night's sleep last night. We're only waiting for the rest of my partial crew, and my love, and . . . well, there will be two pairs of lovers aboard.'

Cleve smiled with genuine delight. 'Is Lahri coming?'

'Lah—' Barke stared at him, his mouth forming an increasingly larger O. 'So *that's* the way it is! I *thought* she seemed concerned beyond casual interest! I'd never have guessed. Hm . . . but she *is* a woman . . . I guess . . .' His smile became a sly grin before he sobered. 'No, I mean someone else, a friend of yours. That slavegirl, what's her name from Rivshar – did she tell you she had a lover?'

'Sovane? A lover? No, she said only that – *not the prince!*'

Barke bobbed his head. 'None other. Prince Reven himself. Oh, we'll be a prize crew of desperadoes, Cleve. If Their Majesties put all the disappearances together – why, every ship in the Sharnese navy will be out after us!'

Cleve groaned. 'You know I'm ready, Barke. I appreciate it far more than I can express, but – this looks very much like a voyage that will end in all our deaths. Surely we can't outrun warships.'

'Well . . . I can perhaps teach them a thing or three about sailing,' Barke said, grinning.

He cocked his head as feet came along the companionway. He and Cleve looked up; the door opened to admit Sovane of Rivshar and a slender, beardless fellow of medium height with a great deal of reddish-brown hair. Both of them wore long, dark cloaks, the hoods now thrown back. Cleve was introduced to His Royal Highness, Reven, Prince of Sharne.

'Are you quite sure you know what you're doing, Your Highness?' Cleve asked. 'Pardon me, but . . . well, this is very romantic, but . . .'

'Call me Reven,' the young prince said. 'Of course I know what I'm doing. You've met my mother!'

Cleve smiled without comment. Yes, from what he'd heard and now seen of Queen Kelas, he could understand Reven's being willing to leave like a thief in the night. But – was he truly in love with his slavegirl paramour? No convenient king's daughter stolen from home was Sovane; she was a slave, born of slave parents. There was at least no question about her feelings; she was positively glowing.

When she gave Cleve a hug of gratitude for his part in bringing all this about, he saw, over her shoulder, the anxious look the prince gave them. *Yes, Reven appears to be in love! If she hugs me a moment longer, I'll be challenged!* Cleve disengaged her.

There were other footsteps as crewmen boarded; Cleve had heard the sounds of loading most of the afternoon. Reven and Sovane left with Barke, to be shown to their quarters.

And Cleve looked up at the cloaked woman in the cabin doorway. He snapped to his feet with a glad cry: 'Lahri!'

She came quickly to him, hard against him, and for a moment they held each other in grateful silence.

'Are you coming?' he asked at last.

The answer was in her eyes as she looked up into his. She shook her head slightly, sadly. 'No. I cannot leave Sharne. Things will be very bad here, soon, and I am one of the few Her Majesty respects. I must stay, Cleve. Will – will you be back?'

He gazed down at her, and his mouth twisted into a helpless little smile. 'Will I? I can't say, Lahri. No, that isn't fair. Probably not. I . . . doubt we'll ever see each other again.'

'You and your honesty! Couldn't you *lie*?' Abruptly her wide mouth stretched into a smile. 'But we will, my love! I have it on the very best authority!' And when he said nothing, questioning her with eyes and brows, she added, 'The Starpowers. My friends, among the "lesser" sorceresses of Sharne who hate the queen and ally with me – without any notion that I have no power at all other than to catch thoughts, now and then. They see you in Sharne's future, and in mine. It was strange, almost amusing, my love, except that my heart was leaping. Two witches arrived almost simultaneously today, to tell me the same thing – and they had been at their spells independently!'

He squeezed her against him. And Queen Kelas had said she'd lose her children through him – and already Reven was aboard! 'All right, then, I believe it, Lahri. Perhaps I will be back. Perhaps tomorrow, as a prisoner or a corpse! Surely we can't leave here without half the navy being after us within minutes, or at the most, hours.'

She laughed the laugh he loved; a crystal-clear mountain stream, rippling happily over the rocks it washed smooth. 'Oh? Well, that will depend on Her Majesty's Starpower, not her regal authority. Is she more powerful than three witches working in unison in my home – right now? We shall see! Even now it gathers, my darling – the thickest fog to envelop the docks of Sharne in years!'

'Fog? Can sorcery control the elements?' And as soon as he'd asked, he knew the answer: Yes, within limits, for on Andor sorcery was elemental. Doralan Andrah's memories told him that, very positively. He began to smile, seeing the hope he had pretended to see before, and again he squeezed her lithe form tightly. 'Lahri – I want you to make me a promise.'

She looked up at him, and a little frown creased her brow. 'You are very serious. I'd promise you anything, you know that. But—'

'The hurt it causes will pass, and it is best.'

'I was warned,' she said softly, 'that you will ever place reason above emotion, even with me. You want me to go now.'

'Mind-reading again, Lahri? No, I don't want you to leave. But . . . I know you must. Go home, take care not to be seen, and stay there. Whatever happens, you can't help. If you won't come along, you can only lose by staying. If I'm indeed to escape and return to Sharne – I want to find you very alive, Lahri, and not in a dungeon.'

She seized his head and drew it down to kiss him fiercely. Then she stepped back to gaze at him a moment, studying his face, his powerful body. Then she whipped her long cloak about her and left, walking rapidly. The cloak rustled susurrantly, like muffled sobbing.

Cleve stood looking at the empty doorway when she'd gone, wondering about love, and logic.

Chapter Twenty-Four

The Fight in the Fog

Cleve went to look out the port; perhaps he could see Lahri.

He could see nothing!

The harbor of Sharne was already well-shrouded with fog, and it was whirling, thickening, even as he looked. The lights ashore were hazy, yellowish nebulae. A questing tendril of the chill, pearly stuff reached in to finger him. He slammed the port's wooden cover.

He knew the crewmen of *Bluerover* were being as silent as possible, but to him, belowdecks, every step, every thump, every creak of wood and lines and tackle seemed loud enough to carry to Orisana.

Then there *were* loud voices, one female. As he strode across the cabin he was glad that they were not on deck.

'But, my darling, we *talked* about leaving,' Barke was saying, in a helpless, almost wheedling voice. 'Half your clothes are aboard, and surely over half your jewels, and—'

'But tonight! Like thieves!' The girl who stood in the passage with her back to Cleve stamped her foot. 'This is *awful!* You're *kidnapping* me!'

'Be reasonable, Sulky. We—'

'Don't call me that!' Her voice rose to new shrillness.

'I'm sorry, darling – you've always loved it. Anyhow, we've *got* to go tonight. We—'

'Why? Why tonight, Barke? Why not as we planned?'

Cleve moved up behind her; he'd no idea what she looked like, face or form, so muffled was she in the thick cloak with its flung-back hood, glistening with droplets of the heavy fog outside.

'Who is this loud-mouthed wench, Captain?' he asked, in a loud voice, and he got in a wink at Barke's surprised face before the girl spun around. She was very young, very pretty, with red-brown hair drawn back into what would have been a ponytail on Earth, save that one seldom saw them bound with a gem-encrusted band of gold. Her eyes flashed at him.

'How dare you, you lout! Get out of here!'

'There's a great fog, Captain, and I think we're all aboard. Shall I take care of this?' Cleve jerked his head at the young woman.

'Uh – Andrah—'

'*This!* Barke, I want this man—'

'Yes,' Barke said hurriedly, squeezing past them and hurrying up the companionway. 'Take care of her! I'm needed on deck!'

Cleve smiled at her. 'If I were he, I'd turn you up and spank you until you promised to act properly respectful,' he said. 'We must leave tonight, because Barke said so. He's captain – isn't he also captain of your heart?'

She was busy looking extremely shocked; her eyes staring, her pretty little mouth working helplessly. Then she frowned: 'What?'

The phrase didn't exist on Andor, he realized; he'd mixed Earthly slang into his Andorite speech. 'You're lovers, aren't you? You've chosen him as lord and master? And here he is in deadly danger, trying to slip out of port on a foggy night like this – and you yowling! If we're caught, you'll be taken back and scolded by your irate parents, no doubt. And what do you think will happen to Barke? Well? Can't you talk, girl?'

He watched as a tear raced down her soft cheek to her chin. It quivered there, lengthening, before dropping off onto the front of her cloak. Her lip quivered; she looked stricken.

'Yes . . . you're right . . . but you've no right . . . I've never been talked to like this before . . .'

'It's past time, isn't it?' he asked, but now his voice was less stern, and he spoke more softly.

She nodded without speaking. Then: 'Who are you?'

'My name is Doralan Andrah, of Elgain. Who are you?'

She'd looked as if she were about to make a sudden movement, her eyes wide and bright. Now she frowned again.

'Don't you know?'

He shrugged. 'I know you're Barke's one and only love,'

he said, using words guaranteed to soothe the savage female breast.

She shook her head in wonder; then she made the sudden movement, thrusting herself against him. Her arms went around him. 'But I have wanted to meet you. You are Barke's hero – and mine, and I thank you, oh, I thank you for saving his life, Doralan! I am his 'Sulky.' Sharnan Selka.'

'Sharnan Sel – *Princess Selka*?'

'Of course. Didn't you know? Now you do, though, don't you? You see why we had to creep away like this. And do you know what I wore for him tonight, just for him? Look.' She stepped back, pulling open her cloak, and it was Cleve's turn to stare.

Beneath the cloak the Princess of Sharne wore the suit sewn from Orimor pelts; the suit made for Cleve by Jaire and the women of Oridorna. It was too tight in the chest; she had that from her bosomy mother. And suddenly he knew, and even more than before he wanted to see this girl spanked; wanted to do it himself.

Barke had waited two days for Lahri's answer, he'd said. Yes, while Lahri consulted another witch, who consulted her smoke and perhaps divined that no graem was needed; Princess Selka was already in love with the freedman named Barke. Then, she must have consulted the girl herself. A romantic idiot, unthinking of the terrible danger, this pretty girl of eighteen with her tear-streaked face had thought how nice it would be for Barke to prove his love by bringing her back an Orimor pelt . . .

'Get into that cabin,' Cleve snapped, 'and stay there. I mean, stay there, and be still! If you come out or squeak or even poke your head out, it'll be me pounding your backside, not Barke, and by Daron I'll use a length of salt-crusted rope from on deck!'

And he whirled and strode away without looking back to see if she obeyed; he heard the rustle of her cloak. He reached for the ladder – and staggered. The deck had tilted beneath his feet. The ship was moving!

Cleve hurried up on deck.

He coughed, wishing he had a cloak, even Selka's. The

ship, the docks, the ships around them, all were blanketed with fog. It glistened wetly on the deck beneath his buskined feet, it made invisible the lights of the city they were leaving. A mast but ten feet away was only a shadow in the writhing gray. It swirled, tendrils like fingers spinning and locking together to form an ever-thicker shroud of shining wet. He stepped back as someone hurried past, shouting:

'We're discovered! Captain – we're discovered! They're boarding!'

Cleve slapped his hip; he'd taken off both sword and sidsorn pouch long ago, in midafternoon, and had not bothered to buckle them on again. He hurried after the man who was already vanishing into the fog.

'I'm Andrah, Barke's friend,' he said, and had snatched the man's scimitar from its sheath and was rushing back before the fellow could turn to squint at him.

Cleve moved at a long-legged, rapid walk along the deck, shining wet. The fog caressed his cheek with wet fingers, seemed to clutch at him; closed in behind him. Ahead of him a light bobbed, and he heard the ring of steel, and a cry. He ran, fog curling in white tendrils about his leg.

He saw them, dark shapes at the bow; Barke of course was astern, striving to get his ship out of her berth and into the open sea. These shapes were helmeted, and he recognized the spikes atop the helmets: the Queen's Own. He did not stop to count; there were several. Barke had said he was short of men, and surely the sailors of *Bluerover* were busy. He was even shorter of men now; the Sharnese soldier with the lantern was bending over a dark form on the deck, holding his light close while he shoved his sword into it more than once. Cleve swung, rather than thrust, and felt the jolt to his arm even as he heard the solid chunking sound. His blade bit, and bit deep and hard. The man howled. His lantern went flying and his sword rattled on the deck. Cleve raced after the lantern as the man dropped.

It had struck the deck and lay there, threatening to spill over onto the planking at any moment. True, the fog was just short of being a light rain, and the deck was very wet.

The burning oil of the lamp would not notice that; it would flow, and continue burning. Cleve started to reach for it.

His peripheral vision caught the movement, the glint of steel; the man had been four or five feet away, and Cleve had not seen him! Hurling himself sidewise, he grunted when he hit the deck. He heard the sword bite into the planking where he'd been; then he was scrambling up and aiming a mighty kick at the burning oil lantern.

It sloshed onto his buskin, burning there harmlessly.

Cleve had no time to worry about a singed boot. He jerked his eyes from the flying lantern to the faceless man in the swirling brume before him. The fellow had gotten his blade out of the deck with little difficulty and was rushing, his scimitar extended. Even as he reflexively used his own scimitar to beat at the approaching blade, Cleve heard the lantern reach the end of its flight – with a splash. He'd saved the ship from fire; now there was the matter of the Queen's Own.

Without the sorcerous fog he'd have had little chance. Aided by its opalescent veil, he'd be a demon who struck fear into them before he struck blood from their bodies. Only the spiked helmets identified them; he could see them in the cold gray wreaths. First beating aside his attacker's blade, Cleve tripped the man as he rushed by. And chopped down into his body as he crashed to the deck. Cleve paused long enough to take his helmet and pull it on. If he could see only shapes with spiked helmets, so could the Sharnese soldiers, now their lantern was gone. But only he knew that every spike was an enemy.

He moved into the writhing gray wetness, feeling its chill kiss on his face and limbs; already his clothing, the tunic he'd found and donned in Barke's cabin, was sodden. But he was not chilled; his exertions saw to that. He waded through it, seeking heads with spikes.

One came. 'Layth? Is that you? What happened to the lant—' The man's question became a scream as Cleve thrust hard at his bulking shape. Yanking back his sword, he thrust again. The guardsman fell, and the man just behind him could not be taken by surprise.

His scimitar arced up and down and Cleve met it desperately with his own curved blade. There was a terrific clang of steel on steel, and he felt the blow, and the give – and then his hand was snapping up, with nothing to strain against. He held only a sword hilt connected to two or three inches of sheared-off steel. He heard the other sword strike the deck along with most of his own blade, and he moved fast.

The Sharnese soldier had not yet jerked his sword up into position when Cleve's arms went around his waist. His knee jerked savagely up. The scream ripped at his ear and rang there for minutes. But the Queen's Own corpsman was dropping, and Cleve bent to knock off his helmet and slam the hilt of his broken sword down on the back of the man's head. He felt along his arm until he found the dropped sword, ribboned with low-swirling fog.

As he grasped it and paused, panting as he knelt, striving to pierce with his stinging eyes the heavy brumous blanket all about him, he heard another yell. Another – and a splash, and a second, and a third.

The ship was moving out; the gangplank or whatever the guardsmen had thrown across to form a bridge – it had grown suddenly too short as the ship moved from beneath it. It had dropped into the water, taking with it at least two of the Queen's Own. Cleve grinned in the darkness, wolfishly; an ugly expression, a savage grimace. There was none to see. He rose to his feet and started forward.

Another cry; a ring of steel on steel; a gagging sound. Ahead of him a voice called, 'That's one less of them, Barke – uh! I've just stumbled over one! He's all blood!'

The lantern man, Cleve thought, and started in that direction. Then a voice spoke from just behind him: 'Surrender, Queen's Own scum, or I'll spit you like a rib roast!'

Cleve spun to see the sword backed up by a shadowy hulk in the fog – a hulk without a spike atop it.

'It's Cleve,' he said. 'Doralan Andrah! I've got this helmet on so they can't – look out!'

And he lunged to the man's left, barely escaping his point, to parry the chopping attack of a guardsman. Strange; the deck was wet and rolling, but the fog seemed to be dissipating. It crept away in ragged gray ribbons. Again he caught a rapidly descending blade on his own, and this time he let his arm go down with it, lessening the force of the blow. Then he exerted the muscles of the powerful body of Doralan Andrah, jerking up arm and sword, hurling aside the guardsman's scimitar, chopping into his neck. The camail gave; then flesh, and the man's scream became bubbling noises. He fell. Somewhere nearby, another was falling before another sword.

And Cleve could see. He could see the body at his feet, its twisted face, and he jerked his eyes from it. He could see the grinning seaman a few feet away; the man who'd challenged him. And other sailors, and other bodies.

No standing man wore a spiked helmet.

They were out of the fog, and the boarders were stopped. Not until considerably later did Cleve stop and count, to be amazed: He had waded through that dripping, clutching fog like a hungry tiger on a moonless night, and he had slain five faceless men.

Astern there was only the fog enshrouding the harbor to frustrate any thought of pursuit. Ahead was the open sea, glistening brightly beneath three moons, lapping at *Bluerover*'s sides as her prow sliced through the fogless night.

Cleve shivered without being cold; even when sorcery was on one's side, it was a shuddery, fearsome thing.

'North,' Barke bellowed. 'Head her north, to Elgain!'

'Where?'

'Elgain, Elgain, Elgain!' And Barke laughed.

Cleve laughed, too, standing on the wet-glistening deck in a torn tunic and buskins – one charred – holding a dripping sword in his big fist. He was a fugitive, on a ship commanded by a fugitive, and below were a fleeing prince and a stolen princess. Ahead was the open sea, to be challenged by a ship with one great sail and a tiny one, little more than a bowsprit, extending out over the waters. He was leaving behind a woman who vowed he'd be back; perhaps he'd see her again; perhaps he would not. Up there, somewhere in the alien sky, was Sol, and Earth, and he doubted that he'd ever see either again.

Earth was Robert Cleve's home, and he was not Robert

Cleve, but Doralan Andrah, and Doralan Andrah's home was in Mor of Elgain. He was going home, and he echoed Barke, laughing into the clear night.

Also available from Magnum Books

ANDREW J. OFFUTT

Messenger of Zhuvastou

In hot pursuit of his beautiful 'fiancee', Earthborn playboy Moris Keniston arrives on the mysterious and hostile planet Sovold. Before he can sample its violent lifestyle and bizarre terrain, or combat the amoral whims of its courts (and blue-haired courtesans) he needs to adopt a suitable disguise.

So, with shaved head and skin dyed beige, he dons the yellow-crested helmet and green cloak of a Messenger of the mighty empire of Zhuvastou. Armed only with a heavy sword he is ready to set out on his urgent quest . . .

The Castle Keeps

The Andrews' hilltop home has become a fortified castle. Jeff Andrews has only ancient weapons to protect his isolated family from the ravages of roving bands of 'rippers'.

The Caudills in the city seem more secure in the protection of their sealed-up apartment building. But they too are gripped by terror, struggling against the hardships of their artificial environment and the dangers that lurk outside.